The kiss was surprisingly gentle...

Miranda stared blindly into his face, eventually causing the Duke of Eversley to grow alarmed. He cursed himself for having so assaulted her innocence, yet he experienced an odd exultation at having awakened her to a sense of herself. For at the last, she had responded ever so slightly.

"You will probably catch my cold, you know," she said gravely. "And it would serve you right. You have treated me quite shabbily."

"Indubitably," he responded. "Must I beg your pardon?"

"You should, perhaps, were I not to blame for what just happened."

"I see," he remarked in a colorless voice. "Then my first suspicions were correct. You *did* set out to entrap a duke!"

THE TORPID DUKE

PAULINE YORK

TORONTO • NEW YORK • LONDON
AMSTERDAM • PARIS • SYDNEY • HAMBURG
STOCKHOLM • ATHENS • TOKYO • MILAN

This book is dedicated with all my love to Steven,
who has a keen appreciation of the absurd.

Published September 1986
ISBN 0-373-31012-9

CHAPTER ONE

"I AM WAITING, my dear," said the rector's maiden sister, "for your explanation."

In dismay, Miranda Waincourt faced the rigid countenance of the lady standing before her, who was attired in forbidding black bombazine, her steel-gray hair pulled up from her scrawny neck and tightly secured in an uncompromising bun. A black bonnet completed the funereal cast. Eyebrows so thin as to be almost nonexistent rose in haughty disbelief as Miss Charity Graves fixed Miranda with nearly colorless pale blue eyes.

"Surely you can assert some control over your misbegotten younger siblings? Mark my words, they will grow to be as reprehensible as their father, God rest his soul, who flung his life foolishly away on an ill-advised wager. Imagine a man of his years riding a green colt in a race from here to Bridingwell in a downpouring rain, and all because Jasper Tonbridge impugned his honor. Disgraceful, I say. But what could be expected of a Waincourt? Fools, the lot of them. Did I not say as much to Millicent Hargrove when first she tossed her cap at him? But no, she would have none of it. Won her heart, she said. That's what comes of read-

ing romances. And what did it get her but five thankless offspring and an early grave.''

Miranda Waincourt, who took exception to being
thought of as either a misbegotten or a thankless offspring, bit her tongue to keep from delivering the
sharp retort that sprang to her lips. Even so, she was
obliged to lower thick lashes to hide the flash of emerald-green eyes.

That she in part agreed with the acid-tongued spinster was all that kept her temper rigidly in check. How
many times had she herself condemned her feckless
father for having left them in the lurch? Henry Waincourt, Earl of Waring, had been a charming rogue
with a glib tongue and the maturity of a schoolboy.
His only virtues had been a sincere devotion to his
fragile wife and a careless affection for his three sons
and two daughters. That he had not gambled away his
entire fortune and the legacy of his eldest son—who
was even then upholding his father's devil-may-care
reputation at Oxford—was only because of his un-
timely demise at the ripe age of four and forty.

That was eighteen months before the present confrontation of Miranda with the old dragon Charity
Graves, and Miranda had since been struggling to put
in order the precarious affairs of her father's estate
and check the harum-scarum escapades of her three
youngest siblings. Of Henry Waincourt the younger
there was rarely word. Following his father's funeral,
he had removed himself promptly to Oxford to continue his studies, after having delivered a brotherly
buss upon Miranda's cheek and a blithe ''You shall do
famously, m'dear, as you have always done.''

Miranda, who had taken the management of the household upon herself at the age of fifteen when her mother had succumbed after the birth of her younger daughter, had assumed the full running of the estate with hardly a demur. After all, she was well acquainted with her father's namesake, and Henry Waincourt, at one and twenty, promised fair to become the same ne'er-do-well that seemed the separate destinies of the earls of Waring. Only their propensity for marrying well-endowed heiresses had kept Groves, the family seat, from falling to rack and ruin. And now, in Miranda's capable hands, the estate was beginning to experience a new prosperity, which owed itself to astute farm management and the growing fame of the Waincourt horses.

Miranda, beset with financial worries, the decisions involved in running the estate and the burden of rearing three spirited younger siblings, had no wish to add the ill will of the surrounding gentry to her list of difficulties. She thus assumed, with difficulty, a polite smile and calmly urged her visitor to be seated.

"Now, my dear," began Miss Graves as she settled herself in the caffoy-covered wing chair near the Adams fireplace and turned her peculiarly colorless eyes upon Miranda. "What do you intend doing about my figwort? You know how highly prized is my herb garden. To think my poor dears should be so brutally savaged."

Miranda carefully folded slim hands in her lap, wondered briefly if the foibles of her brothers and sisters would one day drive her to murder, and leaped into the breach.

"Allie has been warned about Hannibal's predilection for consuming all that comes within his reach," she began in a reasonable voice. "And, indeed, I do beg your pardon for the damage inflicted on your herb garden. Rest assured Allie will be punished and Hannibal properly restrained."

"Alicia stands in need of mature guidance. She should be made to care for a more suitable pet. Nor should she be allowed to roam the countryside attended only by a fractious billy goat. I am thinking only of her best interests, my dear. Either you get rid of the goat and hire a proper governess or I fear I shall have to see that Sir Percival hears of this latest outrage."

Miranda stiffened in alarm.

"But, Miss Graves, Allie is very attached to Hannibal. Indeed, because she has been often ill since infancy, I fear it would do great harm to take Hannibal away from her now that she is gaining strength. And the fresh air and sunshine can only do her good. Surely you see that."

"Nonsense," said the spinster with a prim shake of her head. "The child needs discipline if she is not to become a complete hoyden. You will see to my demands, Miranda dear, or I will go to the magistrate."

Sir Percival, Miranda reflected bitterly, would greatly enjoy the old lady's tale. He was certainly no friend to the Waincourts. She had flatly refused to wed the middle-aged widower, who wished only that his half-grown brood might have a mother to care for them, and no doubt he would greatly relish the opportunity to take her to task. He would order Miranda to put poor Hannibal out of the way just to spite her, and this she could not do. Nor could she afford the probable fine should she refuse. Ah, well, better to soothe the enraged spinster.

She turned an appeasing eye upon the indignant Miss Graves.

"Indeed, Miss Graves, I am not insensitive to the wisdom of your well-meant advice. It is time Allie had a governess, and I shall see to it directly, I promise you. And I shall see to it also that Hannibal remains on the grounds. He will not trouble you further."

Miss Charity Graves sniffed and unfolded her long frame from the soft confines of the chair.

"Very well, my dear," she said in cold triumph. "I suppose I must be satisfied with these assurances. But should that creature invade my property one more time, I shall not be so generous," she added with a pale glint in her eyes. "Well, good day. I know we shall see you in church on Sunday. Dr. Graves so looks forward to having you there. He is not completely indifferent to you, my dear. And it would be such a relief, I know, to have your burdens shouldered by a capable man. I shall do my best to further your cause with my dear brother. He could do worse, after all. And you are fast approaching the regrettable position of being upon the shelf, so to speak."

"My dear Miss Graves," Miranda said in an ominously quiet voice, "I am but three and twenty: hardly at my last prayers. And were I desirous of entering into matrimony, I should not dream of depriving your esteemed brother of his bachelorhood. Do not, I pray you, put yourself out on my account."

The rigid contours of the spinster's face threatened to crack as Miss Graves emitted a peculiar twitter that was meant to pass as a chuckle. "No, no, my dear. I shall not mind a subtle nudge now and then. We spinsters must stick together, must we not?" And with a last covetous glance at the tasteful decor of the Green Saloon, Mistress Graves departed on another of her charitable calls about the neighborhood.

No sooner had the door closed behind her caller than Miranda had picked up her skirts and bounded up the stairs for the nursery. On her way she was accosted by a freckle-faced youth of about ten years who regarded her with open curiosity. His straight red hair fell carelessly across his forehead, and his nankeens bore evidence of a recent foray through mud and wet grass.

"Have you seen Allie?" Miranda asked as she hurried by.

"What's she done now, Sassy?" the stripling queried with the recklessness of youth.

Miranda halted in mid-stride and wheeled to impale her younger brother with an ominous eye. "I'll thank you not to call me by that name, Bertram Waincourt. Where is your sister?"

"Must be somethin' awful to set you off like that," the boy observed. "Oh, well. I'm no talebearer, mind you, but I saw her heading toward the pond with a fishing rod."

"Was Hannibal with her?"

"Well, naturally," he replied with the air of one who cannot be bothered with absurdities.

"You will go and fetch her and Hannibal to me at once," commanded his sister.

As Miranda watched the angular frame of her young brother retreat down the stairs, her brow puckered in a worried frown. Perhaps the old busybody was right, she thought with a weary sigh. The boys were getting out of hand. Not only did her youngest brother run around looking like a stable hand, but Kit also was showing a lamentable tendency to ape the manners of an uncouth set of young bloods who fancied themselves up to every rig. Only last week her sixteen-year-old brother had taken a dare to ride his hunter up the squire's front steps. Only the fact that Robbie, the squire's eldest son, was in on the dare had saved Kit from certain ostracism by the local gentry.

"Miranda, dear, you mustn't frown. It causes wrinkles, you know."

The tall, slender girl wheeled to meet the myopic gaze of her father's eldest sister. The plump, matronly figure attired in the puce brocade of an earlier generation might have startled a stranger. But Miranda hardly noticed the wide hoop and panniers of her aunt's outmoded dress. Not even the ungainly horsehair wig, which attained breathtakingly grandiose heights and housed a menagerie of stuffed birds, could evoke a gasp of dismay from the distraught girl. Miranda had grown immune to Aunt Agatha's eccentricities since her arrival in the Waincourt household some dozen years earlier.

"Have you decided what you will wear to the Davenforths', dear?" asked the elderly lady.

"What? Oh, wear. No, no, Aunt Agatha," replied her niece distractedly. "I shan't be going. Something has come up."

"Not going? But of course you are. Really, Miranda, how can you hope to meet eligible young men when you refuse to go out?"

"I am not interested in meeting eligible young men," returned Miranda on a note of exasperation. Really, it was amazing how everyone seemed bent on marrying her off. "And you know I cannot leave Groves for a fortnight. Who would look after the boys?" The very thought of what could happen in her absence sent cold shivers down her back.

"Who, indeed. Why am I here if not to care for you and the children? Or perhaps you think I am too old. Yes, and useless, too."

Immediately Miranda's soft heart responded to the note of injured pride in the old lady's voice. She placed a comforting arm about her aunt's shoulders and impulsively hugged her.

"Oh, no, Aunt. You know how I depend on you. But Hannibal has raided Miss Graves's herb garden again, and she threatens to take us before the magistrate. You know I cannot allow that. Sir Percival would like nothing better than to see me in the wrong. To fend her off, I have promised to hire a governess to oversee Allie. And Hannibal must be kept on a halter. So you see, I simply cannot leave at this time."

"Fiddlesticks, Miranda. These are not insurmountable obstacles. You know I have long deplored your insistence on instructing Allie and the boys yourself. 'Tis time the boys were sent to school. And much as I mislike having to agree on anything suggested by that viper-tongued old woman, I must do so in this instance. Allie shall have her governess."

"Do you know of a likely candidate, Aunt Agatha?" Miranda asked in some trepidation.

"Indeed I do." The old lady fairly beamed with some secret that she was obviously eager to divulge. "It seems Mrs. Pendergrass's youngest gel is coming out this season, and they have no further need of their governess's services. They did not like to turn her off without finding her a suitable position and have inquired whether Allie might be in need of her. Naturally, I informed Mrs. Pendergrass this morning that you handled all such matters and would call on her as soon as was convenient, this afternoon being the most likely."

"Oh, Aunt! How very clever of you to solve one of my problems so quickly. Of course I shall immediately call on Mrs. Pendergrass."

"And you will go to Applegarth?" her aunt prodded gently. "Groves will survive a fortnight without you, you know."

"Aunt Agatha," Miranda said with tender amusement, "are you implying I am a managing female?"

"You know you are, my dear," replied her aunt with a fond smile. "Lud knows you have had to be. You deserve a husband and a home of your own. Or, if your brother weds, would you spend your life looking after his children—if his wife allowed it? I cannot like to see you throw away all your prospects. Of course, you could change your mind about Sir Percival," she added with an air of profound innocence.

"Or perhaps Dr. Graves could be brought up to scratch. He does seem interested."

"Oh, Aunt!" Miranda laughed. "Surely things are not yet come to such a pass. I have a comfortable competence of my own, after all, thanks to Grandmama. I should simply set up housekeeping on my own."

"Miranda, you know that would never do. No respectable woman would live by herself. It just is not done, despite what your Mrs. Wollstonecraft writes."

"Then I should have you to live with me, my dearest aunt."

"Stop such nonsense at once. You cannot wish such a life for yourself. Am I not example enough to deter you? No, Miranda, it simply will not do. You must not throw away this golden opportunity to meet men of your own station. Say you will go to Applegarth."

Miranda, torn between her overpowering sense of duty and a sudden longing to escape for just a short time her beloved Groves, stood indecisively for a time. Lady Tess's invitation had come as a surprise. Miranda had not seen much of her cousin since her mother's death, when she had had to make it clear to the young matron that there was no hope of Miranda's joining her in London to make her come-out as they had planned for her to do on her seventeenth birthday, for Miranda had become the lady of the manor with all the responsibilities entailed therein. Tess had urged her on innumerable occasions since her coming of age to forgo those responsibilities and seek a life of her own, which had ever meant in her matchmaking cousin's mind the felicities of marriage, a state for which Miranda had long since come to believe she was ill suited. She had had the running of her own life for too long to wish suddenly to give it over to a man who would no doubt regard her as a helpless female incapable of anything more complicated than bearing his children and running his household. She would not be commanded or bullied or condescended to. But Tess, wonderfully content with her own wedded bliss, could not but view her cousin's spinsterhood as a tragedy that must somehow be averted. Thus Miranda had read her cousin's invitation with no little suspicion.

There had been the promise of much gaiety. There would be riding, picnics beside the lake, routs, and perhaps even a ball. But what had appeared most ominous was Tess's blithe gossip concerning three arrogant and very eligible bachelors whom Tess had heartlessly labeled the Three Inconquerables, for they had sworn never to wed. "So you see, dear Cousin," Lady Tess had written, "you need not fear to lose your independence. For Eversley, Chomney and Pulvney will be the only unattached men present, and even I have given over all hope that they will ever succumb to parson's mousetrap. While they are all charming and a welcome addition to any gathering, they are considered quite beyond the touch of even the most determined mama with a marriageable daughter. Do please come, Miranda. I so long to have you here. After all, when was the last time you allowed yourself any fun?"

Suddenly it seemed a very long time indeed since she had allowed herself any frivolity. And the picture of spinsterhood painted by her aunt was not one to bring joy to her heart. *Yes. Why not?* she thought, and lifted her head in unconscious defiance. Surely nothing too drastic could occur in just two weeks' time?

"Very well, Aunt Agatha," she said at last. "Should the governess prove to be reliable, I will go to Cousin Tess's. But mind you, Hannibal must be kept out of trouble."

"And so he shall be, my dear. And so he shall be."

Miranda firmly suppressed the flicker of doubt that sprang to life at Agatha's assurances. With a sinking heart but a sudden unshakable determination that go she would, Miranda hurried off to her chamber to riffle through her wardrobe in search of something suitable to wear at her cousin's house party.

CHAPTER TWO

"IT IS ALL VERY WELL for you to *say* Eversley will be here, Charles. But you know as well as I how little we can depend upon it. Rest assured he will be too fatigued for such a strenuous outing as an intimate gathering of friends."

Sir Charles Davenforth grinned affectionately at the dainty figure of his wife, adorable in her pale blue muslin gown trimmed in white lace. One tiny foot beat impatiently against the flowered pattern of the Aubusson rug that graced the breakfast room at Applegarth. Pale blond curls framed the perfect oval of her face, and blue eyes the color of cornflowers held a twinkle despite the petulant pucker of the perfect rosebud lips.

"My dear Tess, are you not being a trifle hard on poor Evan? After all, when he does honor his friends with a visit, he is unfailingly charming and endears himself to all."

"Oh, quite so," Lady Tess agreed with a grimace that only made her seem more adorable in her husband's fond eyes. "Evan could charm the bristles from a boar, but never was there a more selfish man. He doles his rare visits out as a miser dispenses ha'pennies to the poor. And should he vow he will be one place, one can be sure he will be anywhere but there. 'Oh, but the demands of society are too fatiguing,' he will say, and stifle an insufferable yawn with his hand. Never was there anyone more indolent. He is like a great torpid tomcat with those sleepy eyes that no one can read.''

''Oh, Tess.'' Charles Davenforth chuckled and reached out to pull her onto his lap. ''You know you love Evan, as do we all. Why, there is no one more generous or greater hearted than he. The children adore him, and you cannot deny he has spent a great deal of his time with them.''

Lady Tess regarded her husband's smiling countenance with a suddenly serious mien.

''Oh, yes, Charles. He is perfect with the children. And that is why I would see him happily settled with a loving wife and a nursery of his own. It isn't right that one mercenary female should turn him against matrimony. And 'tis not enough that *he* must swear never to marry, but Chomney and Pulvney must remove themselves from the running as well. The Three Inconquerables indeed! Why, 'tis more than I can bear.''

Sir Charles sighed and shook his head. He well knew that look that glinted in his wife's lovely eyes, and prepared to resign himself and his friend to the inevitable. Yet he could not resist one last attempt to avert his wife's benevolent machinations.

''But what makes you think Miranda and Evan would suit, my dear? While your cousin is well enough looking and has a reasonable enough competence, she is hardly in Evan's usual style. She can make no claim to great beauty. She has never made her come-out. And she is hardly the conformable sort of female who would surround Evan with domestic tranquillity. You know how Evan detests a rumpus of any kind. I fear you are doomed to disappointment in this endeavor."

Lady Tess turned laughing blue eyes on her husband and dimpled delightfully.

"But she is exactly what Evan needs, Charles: someone to jolt him out of his constant state of ennui. He is become much too complacent. And at five and thirty it is more than time for him to wed."

"Nonetheless, my dear, it is Evan's concern. And you know I gave my word that I would never again allow myself to become embroiled in one of your matchmaking schemes, at least where he is concerned," Sir Charles ended with the air of one who has irrevocably terminated a discussion.

Lady Tess studied the suddenly stern face of her husband from beneath long, curling eyelashes. She knew her Charles well and felt it behooved her now to retreat if the battle were not to be lost, for the full scope of her planned campaign went far beyond anything her husband had yet to imagine. It would take all of her resourcefulness, all of her considerable wiles, for if she succeeded, at least one of the Three Inconquerables would have fallen to parson's mousetrap, and all three been taught a valuable lesson of the heart.

It would be her greatest coup yet, she thought as she placed dainty hands upon her husband's hard chest and gazed demurely at his stubborn chin. The thick lashes trembled slightly as though tears threatened, and she spoke in a low, entreating voice.

"You are angry with me, Charles," she said. "You know I cannot bear to have you angry. I am sorry if you think I am trying to make you break your given word. You know I should never think of doing so. You must forget I ever mentioned the subject." She gazed limpidly up into her husband's dark brown eyes and allowed a rather wistful smile to curve her lips.

"Oh, Tess," he said between delighted gasps of laughter, his strong arms enclosing her in a breath-taking embrace. "You minx, you. You are not in the least sorry for your behavior, nor do you have any intention of relinquishing your nefarious scheming."

"Charles, please call on Evan today. Bring him home with you. You need do nothing more. And I promise to leave matters well enough alone should Miranda and he not deal well together. Please, Charles, do this one little thing for me. Is it really too much to ask?"

The laughter in the brown eyes had turned to a quizzical glint as Lady Tess beguiled him with a charming pout. She hardly appeared her one and thirty years, with her smooth rosy cheeks and curved, still-slender figure. Though the fond mother of three hopeful Davenforths, she was yet his elflike Tess. He could deny her nothing.

With a somewhat crooked smile, he pressed a kiss upon her smooth brow and reluctantly set her on her feet.

"Very well, dear heart," he said on a note of resignation. "I shall beard the lion in his den."

"Oh, no, Charles. Hardly a lion. A sleepy pussycat waiting to be awakened. Miranda will be good for him, I promise."

Sir Charles regarded the impish face of his wife with a dubious quirk of a dark eyebrow. Somehow he could not quite picture the six-foot-two Duke of Eversley as a pussycat. Sleepy, perhaps, for the duke's indolence was well known among the members of the ton. Yet had one ever faced His Grace in the ring or across raised swords, one would have grave doubts of the wisdom of awakening the sleepy cat.

Ah, well, there was no dissuading Tess once she had her mind set on a thing, and at least Miranda was well able to take care of herself. He thought of the fiery-headed, green-eyed girl and shuddered. Evan would never forgive him for his part in all this were it to become known. He must tread softly, very softly indeed.

IT WAS THUS with unwonted reluctance that Sir Charles called at the magnificent four-story town house at number five Grosvenor Square to see his oldest and closest friend, the Duke of Eversley.

Though it was long past noon, Sir Charles was not surprised to learn from Eversley's butler that the duke was but recently risen, and would join him in the book room directly. Thus Sir Charles, having accepted the butler's invitation to a brandy, thinking a bracer under the circumstances would not be amiss, was left to peer distractedly at a magnificent tortoiseshell ink-well inlaid with mother-of-pearl that sat upon a contemporary rosewood writing table. While in town, His

Grace was seldom known to leave his bed until after noon, upon which time it was his custom to make a leisurely toilet, followed by an even more leisurely luncheon. It was a rare event indeed to meet His Grace anywhere about town before the fashionable hour of five, when the *haut ton* were wont to display themselves at Hyde Park. It was never his habit to make or receive morning calls, and only his intimates were allowed access to his private chambers before the hour of three. Consequently, there was much speculation about how the duke utilized his time when not being seen at White's, Watier's, Hyde Park or the theater. If he deigned to accept an invitation to a ball, the hostess was assured of a *succès fou*. If he appeared at a rout, a soirée or a musicale, it was considered *un fait accompli*. If he were ever to materialize at Almack's, it would have been considered nothing short of miraculous.

The duke used his reputation for indolence as a means of fending off the legion of toad-eating hangers-on who had made his early accession to the dukedom unbearable. It had stood him in good stead as well among the predatory matchmaking mamas with their simpering debutantes who otherwise would have hounded him to distraction. And, furthermore, it kept at bay his formidable family of four older sisters with their numerous progeny, who tended to view his vast pocketbook as their own.

Not that Eversley was parsimonious. Quite the contrary. He maintained numerous projects for the common good. But none of his endeavors was publicly known, with the result that he was viewed by a goodly number as clutch-fisted—except, of course, in the manner of his public pursuits. He gambled frequently and heavily, but won more often than not. He was generous in the entertainment of his friends and lavish in his dealings with the long line of barques of frailty who had in turn beguiled him to their beds. He was, in short, reputed to be a nonpareil, a top-of-the-trees Corinthian and a rake.

Yet all of this was deceiving, as Sir Charles well knew. Had those acquainted only with his reputation known how he really spent the vast amount of his jealously guarded time, they no doubt would have been astounded. For Evan Westlake, Duke of Eversley, was a scholar possessed of a keen and searching mind. He was addicted to the pursuit of science in its many facets, and to the study of theoretical mathematics most particularly. Naturally, a man could not be expected to rise before noon had he sought his bed but a short time before dawn.

It was in fear that their friend would one day become a total recluse—or would perhaps ruin his health were his secret obsessions given total reign over his life—that his closest comrades took it upon themselves to lure him from his private mania into more healthful pursuits and occasional entertainments. These intimates included Sir Charles Davenforth, the Earl of Chomney, commonly known as Chums, and the Marquess of Pulvney, all determined bachelors with the exception of Sir Charles, who had succumbed at an early age to parson's mousetrap and had flourished in the environment of wedded bliss to the secret delight and envy of his more cynical cohorts.

But none of this was to the point, for Sir Charles had been induced by his well-meaning wife into playing the role of Judas.

It was perhaps an uneasy conscience that caused Sir Charles to start abruptly when the duke's soft drawl broke into his troubled thoughts.

"Rather early for you to be imbibing, isn't it, Charles? Don't tell me you and Tess have had a falling out, for I shan't believe you. Tell me, my man, what troubles you?"

Sir Charles spun around to see the tall form of his friend lounging lazily against the doorframe. He suspected that the smile of welcome he had adopted was foolishly awry, and quickly replaced it with a mock grimace of censure.

"Not the thing to creep up on a man, Evan," he complained, thinking to turn aside his friend's probing with an aggressive front. "You nearly startled me out of a half-year's growth."

The duke strolled casually into the room and halted before his friend, regarding him speculatively. "Might not be a bad thing, old boy," he observed with a slow smile and gently patted Sir Charles's ample girth. "I see that marriage continues to agree with you."

Sir Charles eyed with envy the duke's lean frame, set off to advantage in snug buckskin breeches, knee-high gleaming Hessians with gold tassels, and a green riding coat of Bath superfine, which hugged indecently broad shoulders.

"I could still take you in five rounds. See if I couldn't," he challenged and lifted his big fists to cuff invitingly at the duke.

"No, no, my friend," Eversley rejoined, neatly parrying the baronet's blows. "I should hate to humiliate you. You've grown stout as a bull and slow as an ox. It would be unfair to take advantage of you."

"And you've become as soft as a town beau, Evan, while I've toughened my body with honest labor. 'Tis the country which agrees with me. And 'tis the country for which you have need. Come with me to Applegarth. A fortnight of outdoor pursuits would rid you of your prison pallor and make a man of you."

"Ah, am I become less than a man?" The duke laughed and broke through Davenforth's guard to send an ungentle blow into his friend's midsection.

The baronet grinned broadly, relishing the game the two had played since their rough-and-tumble boyhoods. He caught the uppercut intended for his chin in a viselike grip as the two pitted their strength one against the other. It was not long before they had laughingly conceded a draw. Sir Charles pounded his friend painfully on the back and invited the duke to join him in a libation.

It was a strategical error, for it recalled Eversley to his earlier train of thought.

"Now tell me," he said as he took the crystal goblet half filled with the amber liquid and settled into an armchair across from his friend, "why do I find you glass in hand, an unwonted scowl imbedded in your brow?"

Sir Charles tried not to fidget beneath the duke's amused scrutiny and wished he had not succumbed to Tess's beguiling.

"Let me ponder the problem. What would send my dear Charles into the doldrums?" Assuming a sober mien, the duke rolled his startlingly blue eyes ceiling-ward and pursed his lips thoughtfully. "It must be something to do with your lady wife. Naught else short of an invasion from Bonaparte could upset your usual congeniality," he murmured tantalizingly. "Aha! I have it!" he exclaimed and grinned when Sir Charles jumped guiltily in his chair. "The dear, kind-hearted but unfailingly meddlesome Tess has once more decided 'tis time I was wed. I had previously agreed to come to Applegarth, I believe, for a house party." He watched, interested, as his friend's cheeks turned a dusky red. "She has therefore sent you to fetch me to her that I might meet and fall hopelessly under the spell of her latest protégée. That is it, isn't it, Charles? She feared I would not come, and she has sent you to make sure of me."

Davenforth, who had succumbed to a violent par-oxysm of coughing after having choked on his brandy at the duke's uncannily accurate deductions, wiped streaming eyes with his handkerchief.

"No, no, Evan," he gasped and sucked in a great gulp of air. "How could you accuse me or Tess?"

"Because I know you both so well. Tell me, who is this latest paragon? A simpering beauty just newly arrived on the marriage mart, who has not yet learned of my heartless reputation for snubbing young debu-tantes? I should have thought dear Tess more know-ing than that. Perhaps it is a lovely widow, then, with voluptuous curves and an entertaining wit. I should at least find such an encounter somewhat less boring,'' he ended with a decided leer.

Sir Charles straightened indignantly to fasten offended eyes upon the lounging duke. "Damme! You've no call to be insulting, Evan," he said heatedly. "You make Tess sound like the mistress of a bagnio. You're grown rather too cynical of late, methinks. Or have you forgotten how fond of you my wife has always been?"

"I beg your pardon, Charles." The duke had the grace to look chagrined. "I've become the veriest coxcomb, no doubt, believing every woman's sole intention to be my entrapment. And were I to find a paragon like your own Tess, perhaps I should succumb gladly. Mayhap your lady wife has found just such a candidate for my affections?"

Somehow Sir Charles could not quite see the indomitable Miss Waincourt in the same light as his adorable Tess, but his wife had been positive that Miranda and the duke would suit admirably. He put on an affable face and gruffly denied his friend's suspicions.

"No such thing, Evan. Assure you. 'Tis only a small house party. You know how you tend to bury yourself here. Well, we merely thought it time you got out again. Chums and Jeremy will be there. And the Crenshawes. Lady Horton and her daughter. You remember Marian."

"Indeed," Eversley agreed with an appreciative grin as he recalled his friend's lively young cousin. "She must be sixteen or seventeen now. Quite the young lady. Surely Tess has not picked out a schoolroom miss for my approval.''

''Marian is eighteen and is engaged to an officer in the dragoons,'' Sir Charles replied dampeningly.

''Oh, well, then,'' the duke said irrepressibly, ''I shall be quite safe.''

''And then there is Miranda Waincourt, m'wife's cousin,'' Sir Charles added in an offhand manner. At the sudden quizzical quirk of the duke's arrogant eyebrow, he experienced a sinking feeling. It was then that inspiration came to him. ''A sworn spinster of three and twenty,'' he coldheartedly labeled Miss Waincourt. ''Redheaded, freckled and possessed of only passable looks. Furthermore, she is considered a wholly sensible female, a follower of Mrs. Wollstonecraft, and a believer in the rights of women: one, in short, who would never succumb to the blandishments of a rake such as yourself. So you need not fear her, either. I daresay even you could not engage *her* interest.''

''Hates men, does she?'' queried the duke with a slight yawn.

''Don't know as I'd go that far,'' Sir Charles disclaimed, puckering his brow thoughtfully. ''Let us say that the men in her life have done little to endear her to our sex. Her father was the Earl of Waring, y'know. A charming ne'er-do-well who got himself to an early grave on a dare. The heir promises to be cut of the same cloth. Left her with the running of the family estate. Miranda's had her hands full raising her younger brothers and sister and keeping Groves afloat.''

The duke gave a slight shudder. "A managing female. The worst kind. I do think I must refuse your generous invitation, Charles."

"Well, perhaps you're right, Evan," Sir Charles agreed affably. "Miranda no doubt would prove too much for you to handle. She's a high-spirited filly that don't take well to the bridle. The man hasn't been born yet who could break her to the saddle. Can't blame you for wishing to bow out. Too bad. Tess and the children had looked forward to having you at Applegarth."

Eversley regarded his friend with narrowed eyes. He could not quite subdue a slight prick of resentment at Sir Charles's brash judgement of his prowess with the fairer sex. After all, it was not that he was afraid of the woman. It was simply too fatiguing to deal with the headstrong, forceful type. So unfeminine, too, he thought with an inner grimace of distaste. He preferred the more pliant creatures of the demimonde whose sole purpose was to ease a man's weightier existence. And yet, of late he had been conscious of a vague dissatisfaction with his ordered existence, a feeling of stagnation that his various private pursuits had not altogether routed. He had begun to feel a trifle bored. No doubt Charles was quite right about his needing some time in the country. If only he had not to deal with the inevitable scheming of the adorable Tess and the probable irritation of the managing Miss Waincourt. Better to remain in London far from any unpleasantness that might arise from proximity to the spinsterish cousin.

It was, then, with a sense of having joined the ranks of Bedlam that he heard himself reply to Sir Charles's invitation in the affirmative.

"I shouldn't wish to disappoint Lady Tess or the children, after all. And who knows, I might find some entertainment in attempting to dissuade the redoubtable Miss Waincourt from her aversion to men. What do you think, Charles?"

"I think you would be better off not attempting anything so foolhardy," replied Sir Charles with a look of horror. "She is sure to take you in aversion. You, after all, are reputed to be a rake, much like her father. No, Evan, you will have little success attempting to breach her formidable defenses. She is sure to keep you at arm's length and will treat you with icy formality."

Later the duke was to assume that either he had suffered a momentary aberration or some hitherto unsuspected quirk in his nature had prompted him to pursue the matter to its disastrous conclusion.

"Would you care to wager on that?" he drawled recklessly. "Let us say that neat little bay mare of yours against my Agincourt that in a fortnight's time I shall have the managing Miss Waincourt on the friendliest of terms. She shall even call me 'Evan, darling' before I am through with her."

"Damme, Evan!" Sir Charles exclaimed, his face reddening in indignation. "Miranda don't deserve to be made the object of a wager. I've always been fond of the gel, y'know. She's a right 'un once you get to know her. Besides, Tess'd never forgive me if she found out."

"And who's to tell her? Come, Charles. It's time Tess was taught she cannot meddle in the affairs of others. And I will not dishonor or harm her cousin. A light flirtation—nothing more."

Sir Charles shifted uneasily in his chair. Tess would light into him with a vengeance if she ever found out. And yet...

"Agincourt, y'say? Your gray hunter?" he queried, weakening, and thus set into motion the events that were to seal all their fates.

CHAPTER THREE

MIRANDA EYED the three younger Waincourts, who were lined up before her in impeccable array, or at least impeccable, were one to discount Kit's studied slouch, the somewhat less than immaculate neckcloth tied carelessly about his throat and the several whip thongs thrust through the top buttonhole of his drab driving coat. And surely one could not expect a ten-year-old to keep his shoes unmuddied, or consume seven pieces of toast without dropping just a dab of strawberry preserves on his shirtfront, she observed charitably as she looked fondly at Bertie. At least Allie looked as pretty as a picture in her pink frock with a matching ribbon in her red-gold hair, and one could overlook the vestiges of tears upon the lightly tanned cheeks when one considered how difficult it must be for a little girl barely eight years old to understand why her beloved pet and constant companion must be kept tethered in the stable until his latest transgressions could be forgotten.

Miss Melbourne stood at prim attention behind the two youngest children. At least here one could find no fault, Miranda decided. She had been immediately taken with the soft-spoken governess, whose credentials were impressive and who was able to cope with the youngsters with a firm but amused tolerance. She was a paragon among governesses.

Miranda kissed her young brothers and sister and admonished them, upon peril to life and limb, to stay out of trouble. Then she hugged Aunt Agatha and climbed into the coach where Peggy, the upstairs maid recruited to act as abigail, awaited her. Four prime bloods bred on the Waincourt estate chomped the bits. Tied behind the coach was Aster, Miranda's favorite mount, a dapple-gray mare with long legs and gentle eyes.

Miranda settled with a heavy sigh against the somewhat shiny velvet squabs and discovered, rather to her surprise, that her eyes were dewy. How silly, she chided herself even as she acknowledged an unaccountable feeling that she was somehow irrevocably changing the pattern of her life. She was almost tempted to climb out of the carriage then and there. Instead, she dabbed impatiently at her eyes with the wisp of lace that served as a lady's handkerchief, then vigorously blew her nose. Perhaps this preoccupation with an inexplicable feeling of impending doom was the reason Miranda did not see the figure of a shaggy goat, trailing a frayed rope about its neck, bound with sure instinct across the road in the direction of the rectory.

Miranda found the journey to Applegarth in the neighboring county of Kent exciting at first. She had never been farther than twenty miles from Groves, and she feasted her eyes on the gently rolling countryside. Sternly she quelled any misgivings she might have at her first entrée into society, determined instead to en-

joy her freedom from the cares of Groves come what
may. When she grew weary of gazing out upon the
passing scenery, she leaned her head against the squabs
and tried to sleep.

But the Waincourt travel coach, which had not been
used since before her mama's death, was sadly in need
of new springs as well as refurbishing. It was not long
before every bone in her slender body felt in danger of
becoming displaced. The constant lurch and sway
brought every muscle into play as she struggled to keep
her seat. It was thus with heartfelt relief that she eased
her stiff and sore body from the hateful coach upon
arriving at an inn some dozen miles from Applegarth.

The inn yard was abustle with numerous carriages
of all descriptions on their way to or from London.
Hostlers scurried about the yard changing teams or
catering to the demands of the gentry. Miranda placed
her handkerchief to her nose to ward off the rising
dust and hurried toward the entrance to the inn, her
maid trailing a respectful distance behind her. Her eyes
stinging from the dust and her thoughts on an anticipated dish of tea with perhaps a pastry or two, Miranda failed to see the tall figure of a gentleman
admirably clad in buckskin riding breeches and dark
blue coat of Bath superfine striding out the door.

Amid the confusion of the resultant collision, Miranda was but vaguely aware of two strong arms
sweeping her into a tight embrace. She knew only that
her nose was painfully dashed against a hard obstacle
that bore the pleasant, mingled scents of shaving soap

and tobacco, and that both her arms were imprisoned in a viselike grip. She reacted instinctively.

Afterward she was to regret acting without previous thought. Not only did she grievously hurt the big toe of her right foot as it connected with a hard shin, but the tall gentleman, who proved to be the handsomest man she had ever seen, was most unreasonably put out by the assault on his person. He released her so precipitantly that she almost fell.

"I beg your pardon, ma'am," he drawled acerbically, "for inflicting myself upon your person. Perhaps were you to look where you are going, future such assaults might be avoided."

The embarrassed apology that had trembled upon Miranda's lips trailed away at the man's bored tones. Emerald eyes swept the handsome face remarkable for its veiled look of ennui.

"I assure you I am not in the habit of blundering into people," she said somewhat stiffly and attempted to straighten her bonnet, which had been knocked to the back of her head. In the process she simultaneously dropped her reticule and lashed the stranger's eyes with the ostrich feather that adorned her hat. The gentleman winced, and a low exclamation escaped from between remarkably white teeth. Miranda's confusion was only intensified by the warm rush of blood to her cheeks.

"Oh, I do beg your pardon, sir!" she cried in heartfelt contrition. It was then her eyes fell upon the reticule at her feet. In a convulsive movement she bent to retrieve it just as the gentleman started to do the same.

"Cease and desist, madam," he ordered, missing a third painful encounter with the lady only by grasping her shoulders and holding her at arm's length. "Had you any mercy in that deceptively fragile-appearing form, you would remain perfectly still."

Spellbinding eyes of a particularly brilliant blue held her speechless. Absently she noted raven hair brushed in the casually elegant style known as the windswept look. A long straight nose, high cheekbones, and firm mouth all gave the impression of a man used to having his own way. One small portion of Miranda's brain that still functioned normally categorized him as top-lofty and overbearing. Unaccountably, her pulse began to race.

At last he apparently deemed her sufficiently disarmed and stooped to retrieve the fallen reticule. In a smooth, graceful motion, he straightened to attention, bowed slightly, and languidly offered the lady her property.

"Madam?" he prodded gently when Miranda continued in an apparent trance, her wide-eyed gaze fixed upon his face. At last a glimmer of amusement flickered in the blue eyes. "Madam," he repeated in his rich baritone, "your reticule."

"What?" murmured the lady. "Oh! Yes. Of course. Thank you, sir." Miranda fumbled for the reticule, then stood uncertainly before the tall gentleman. She wondered briefly if her wits were wanting and observed wryly that if all her encounters with town beaux were to be of a similar discommoding nature, she would have a sad time of it at Applegarth.

"Beggin' your pardon, Miss Miranda," her abigail said at her elbow. "The coach is ready to carry us to Applegarth. John Coachman says we'd best be on our way as a storm be threatenin'."

Recalling with a jolt just where she was and in whose presence, Miranda drew in a deep breath and straightened her back. With an effort she gathered her scattered thoughts and, glancing up with a sweet smile, proffered her hand to the gentleman.

"I do humbly apologize," she said in a nearly normal tone. "I am not usually so gauche. It's just that the dust was so bad and I fear my thoughts were on getting inside as quickly as possible. And then when you grabbed me, well, I..." She faltered, her voice dying away as she found that she could not possibly explain why she had behaved in so unladylike a manner as to kick someone she had mistakenly believed to be intent upon assaulting her. Oh, it was too mortifying. She blushed, like a simpering schoolroom miss, she thought disgustedly, wishing she had never left the safe haven of Groves.

"But there is no need to apologize," the gentleman said smoothly, grasping her hand lightly in his own strong one. A disarming smile curved the handsome lips as the gentleman suddenly swept the curly-brimmed beaver from his head and bent over her hand to kiss her knuckles lightly. "A lovely lady need never apologize for anything."

Miranda was suddenly struck by the startling change in his manner toward her. Where before he had been mildly amused and perhaps more than a little bored, he now gazed upon her with an arrested look in the disturbing blue eyes. Now, what was this? she wondered with dawning suspicion.

Suddenly something about the easy charm that he seemed able to turn on at a moment's notice called to mind an image of her roguish father. Even so had he beguiled all around him. She was, she told herself, in the presence of a practiced rake. She pulled her hand quite firmly from the gentleman's and treated him to a cool gleam of emerald eyes.

"How very gallant," she said dryly. "And yet, since I do not fall into that category, I do tender my apologies and wish you a good day, sir." She would have turned then with a brief curtsy and left him, but the gentleman detained her with a lift of an arrogant eyebrow.

"Now, how have I offended you, I wonder," he mused with the air of one confronted with a conundrum.

"You have not offended me," Miranda replied with a level gaze. "I simply prefer plain pounds to Spanish coin. And now I really must be going. I beg you will excuse me."

The gentleman's lips curved in an appreciative smile.

"That's given me some of my own, no doubt," he said. "Are you always so severe with gentlemen desirous of nothing more than exchanging pleasantries? Or is it simply that you have unaccountably taken *me* into dislike?"

Miranda cocked one wary eyebrow and awarded him a dubious glance from the corner of her eye, yet a telltale quiver of her lips betrayed her lively appreciation of the absurd.

"I cannot imagine why my opinion of you should matter to you in the least," she responded pertly. "I do not even know you. Nor is my deportment with gentlemen your affair. And since we have not been properly introduced, it little behooves me to be seen standing here conversing with a total stranger. Once again I beg your pardon and wish you a pleasant day."

With a cool nod of her head, she turned and, grasping the gaping abigail by the elbow, made her escape from the gentleman's disturbing presence.

Once safely ensconced within the coach, Miranda could not resist peeking out the window at the intriguing stranger. She saw the gentleman stride across the yard to a waiting curricle. A pair of magnificent chestnuts waited in the traces, their heads held by a young tiger appareled handsomely in silver and blue livery. The tall gentleman climbed lithely to the driving seat and took up the ribbons. As he waited for the tiger to jump up behind the curricle, he glanced deliberately at Miranda and tipped his hat in her direction, an ironic smile upon his face. Then the curricle swept out of the yard to disappear around a bend in the road.

"Well!" Miranda exclaimed with a furious blush at having been caught spying on the insufferable man. "Thank heavens I am not likely to meet him again." Yet it was some time before she was able to dismiss the image of sleepy blue eyes gazing sardonically into her own.

The threatened storm burst a scant thirty minutes after the Waincourt coach had pulled out of the inn yard. Miranda stared anxiously out at the rain-drenched landscape and wondered whether they should not turn about and weather the storm at the inn. They had left the thoroughfare and now traversed a country road that was growing increasingly treacherous with mud already fetlock deep. The coach swayed drunkenly through deep ruts and bounced over rocks exposed by the downpour. Had not John Coachman been a retainer of many years' standing and noted for his great dependability and skill, Miranda would not have hesitated to call a halt. As it was, she experienced a growing excitement at the thrilling fury of the storm.

The sudden lurch of the ancient vehicle as it struck a rock and nearly spilled over on its side caused the abigail to squeal.

"We shall all be killed," the unfortunate girl wailed and clutched dramatically at her breast.

"Nonsense, Peggy," Miranda scolded, placing a comforting arm around her maid. "John Coachman will get us through."

As though her words had displeased the fickle gods, the coach jolted to an abrupt halt. Miranda and her maid tumbled ignominiously to the floor. Struggling to free herself from a tangle of arms and encumbering skirts, Miranda pulled herself upright and peered out the window.

Torrents of rain lashed against the coach, effectually obscuring her view. With an impatient exclamation, she threw off her hat and wrapped a woolen scarf about her head. Then she thrust open the door and stepped out into the storm.

"Oh, miss!" the abigail cried out in horror. "You'll catch your death!" But Miranda was made of sterner stuff. Ignoring the pleas of her maid, she shoved the door shut and trudged to the front of the coach. Wind whipped her already sodden skirts about her legs, and, ever practical, she was grateful she had chosen to wear for traveling an old worsted carriage dress that had belonged to her mother rather than one of her less old-fashioned gowns.

John Coachman glanced down at her from his seat atop the coach. He showed neither surprise nor consternation at seeing his young mistress wading through the slippery mud. The lass had worked beside him caring for the prime Waincourt cattle in all kinds of weather almost since she had left her leading strings. With a curt nod of his head he gestured toward the cause of their precipitous halt.

Lying on its side some few feet in front of them was a curricle. A tall figure in a many-caped driving coat fought to quiet his frightened, plunging chestnuts. Miranda had time only to recognized the haughty stranger from the inn before she was slipping and sliding through the mud to offer aid.

The horses were in danger of crippling themselves as they fought to free themselves from the traces. The long lines were entangled about the forelegs of one plunging chestnut. In a moment it would be down if its mate were to continue its frenzied pitching. The stranger appeared oblivious to danger as he stepped close to the pawing forefeet and coolly caught the bri-

dle near the bit. With an iron grip he dragged the
leader down. Miranda grasped the bridle of the other
entangled horse and ran sure hands down its quivering neck.

The gentleman flashed a grim look over his shoulder at her.

"Stand back!" he shouted, but the girl merely gri-
maced at him and began to speak soothing words to
the frightened beast whose head she held. In moments it stood trembling beneath her hands, its head
down.

"That's a good baby. There, there. It's all right,"
she crooned and worked her way down the glistening
shoulders to the forelegs.

"Careful!" warned the stranger through clenched
teeth. "That's no lady's hack. Don't press your luck."

"Nor am I accustomed to dealing with ladies'
hacks," Miranda flung back at him, and went about
the business of disentangling the lines. She stood then
and patted the animal's trembling neck. "There.
You're fine now, my beauty," she said and, smiling
demurely into the gentleman's stormy countenance,
led the horse away from the wrecked vehicle.

Miranda tethered the chestnut to a tree and turned
to see the gentleman leading the other horse out. A
slight form huddled in the road a little distance away
caught her eye.

"Your tiger!" she cried and plowed through the
mud toward the boy. The man's long strides outdis-
tanced her. She was surprised to see the gentleman
kneel unhesitatingly beside the still form. Somehow
she had thought he would be like most of the town tu-

lips she had heard of, reluctant to ruin his fine clothes. She watched him probe with sensitive fingers for broken bones. A gash on the boy's forehead oozed blood.

"No bones broken," the gentleman pronounced and sat back on his heels with an audible sigh of relief.

"We must get him into the coach," Miranda said. "He is wet to the skin."

"As are you. What did you think you were doing back there? You might have been killed," he declared acidly as he bent to lift the boy gently in his arms. Miranda walked beside him, aware of a growing weariness and the chill of wet clothes clinging to her body.

"Fiddlesticks! I've been around horses all my life. And this is not the time to argue the proper place for women of delicate sensibilities—of which I have none, I might add. Or so my Aunt Agatha has accused on several occasions. Just how do you come to be in such a fix?"

"We had an unfortunate encounter with a rock," he offered briefly. "The axle broke."

They had reached the coach, and Miranda struggled to open the door. Peggy stared shamefaced as Miranda climbed in and turned to receive the boy tenderly.

"We will take your tiger with us to Applegarth. Can you follow us there? I do not think it is much farther," Miranda added somewhat doubtfully.

"Perhaps an hour or more in this weather," he replied, his gaze quizzical as he took in her streaming hair and sodden clothing. Unconsciously Miranda's pointed chin rose beneath the gentleman's sardonic glance. "Are you always so impetuous, Miss Miranda?" the gentleman queried, a hint of amusement in the rich baritone. "Rescuing strangers is hardly the usual pursuit of gently bred females. 'Twould seem you need someone to take you in hand. Have you no father or brother?"

"I am well able to look after myself, sir," Miranda replied tartly, the emerald eyes widening at the man's audacity. "Indeed, you should concern yourself not with me but, rather, with the welfare of your cattle. They are like to take cold in this weather." The gentleman regarded her with a bemused stare.

"No, you certainly are not of the usual run of females," he murmured as if to himself, and unaccountably Miranda blushed at the curious gleam in his eyes. "But even headstrong beauties with more bottom than brains are like to catch their death at such a wetting." A sudden grin flashed across his face at her stifled gasp of anger. "You had best be on your way."

Then he was gone, leaving Miranda to gape at the closed door, a lingering image of a glint of laughter in startlingly blue eyes adding to her unusually confused state of mind. Briefly, pique at his typically male attitude toward her sex vied with her awakening sense of humor. Really, it was idiotish the way she became flustered whenever she was near the man. Then the unconscious boy stirred in her arms, recalling her to present duties.

"Quickly, Peggy. We must get him dry."

Together they stripped the child of his outer clothing and rubbed him dry with the maid's shawl. Then they wrapped him in a carriage rug. Miranda wiped the blood tenderly from the thin face and bound the gash with strips torn from her maid's petticoat.

Miranda shivered in her own wet clothes and wondered if they would ever see her cousin's house. She did not envy the stranger his ride through the steady downpour. Even with the protection of his greatcoat he would be soaked to the skin long before they reached Applegarth.

He had seemed much different from the indolent gentleman she had encountered at the inn, Miranda reflected. She thrilled anew at the memory of his masterful handling of the fear-maddened chestnuts. After witnessing his quick concern for his servant, she thought she liked him rather better than she had at their first meeting. The disturbing effect of his warm smile and intent gaze as he left her she refused to contemplate. Yet she was conscious of a small tingle of anticipation at the prospect of meeting him again.

Miranda was drooping with fatigue when at last they pulled into the long, tree-lined drive to Applegarth. It was not yet dusk, yet the storm cloaked the Elizabethan mansion in deepening gloom. The house, which formed an E, was fronted by a portico, the roof of which was supported by Ionic columns. Miranda guessed it had been added by some later generation of Davenforths. The bleached bricks were graced with ivy carefully trimmed about the myriad mullioned windows. Miranda had the impression of neat lawns and formal gardens before a cloaked footman opened the coach door and looked with scarcely concealed surprise at the shivering, mud-bespattered young lady within.

"Take the boy," she ordered. "Gently, man. He may be concussed."

When the boy had been taken from the coach and carried inside, Miranda climbed down unaided and hurried toward the figure of her cousin peering out at her from the doorway.

"Miranda, dear," called Lady Tess. "Whatever have you been about? Come in at once!"

"I shall ruin your floors," Miranda said ruefully as she was whisked inside.

"Nonsense. We must get you out of those wet things and into a warm bath. Good heavens! You look a fright. What have you been doing? Rolling about in the mud?"

Miranda laughed, greatly pleased to see her dear Tess again.

"I have had the most delectable adventure, Tess! If only the boy is not seriously hurt," she added on a sober note. "He lay so still in my lap all the way here. I cannot help but fear for him. I should be most grateful if you would summon a doctor for him."

"A doctor has been summoned, ma'am," drawled a lazy voice from behind her, and Miranda whirled about to meet the indolent blue gaze of the stranger.

He had changed into gray unmentionables and a burgundy coat that hugged his broad shoulders to perfection. An immaculate neckcloth tied in the waterfall and bearing a single ruby in its folds admirably set off the gray flowered waistcoat. He wore a single fob, and a quizzing glass was suspended from a black riband about his neck. He was the most elegant man she had ever seen, and Miranda was made suddenly aware of her own muddy and bedraggled appearance.

Her hair hung in sodden strands about her face, which she did not doubt was besmirched with mud. Her woolen skirt clung wetly to her. Miserably she shifted from one foot to the other as a slowly widening pool of dirty water spread at her feet.

"Oh, you are here before us!" she cried in some confusion at his sudden appearance. "Then your cattle are fit, I must assume. I am so glad. I cannot like to see such fine animals injured."

The gentleman's lips twitched in amusement, though his deep voice was properly grave as he answered her medley of observations.

"I made my way cross-country and so cut the distance. And indeed my horses have not suffered greatly from their misfortune. Yet you, madam, stand in danger of taking an inflammation of the lungs. Might I suggest you follow your cousin's advice immediately?"

"But the boy...?"

"Will be properly looked after, I promise you."

"Come along, my dear," urged Lady Tess. "I shall take you to your rooms, and you can tell me all about your adventure with His Grace."

"H-His Grace?" Miranda stammered with a sense of impending doom. Lady Tess regarded her with a mischievous glint of laughter in her blue eyes.

"But did you not know? Evan, how could you be so remiss as not to introduce yourself? Miranda, this is

Evan Westlake, Duke of Eversley. Miss Miranda Waincourt, my cousin.''

"Miss Waincourt," drawled the duke, and bowed over her ice-cold hand. "I feel we are already intimate friends after our previous hazardous and sometimes—er—painful encounters."

Miranda's eyes fell away from his sardonic gaze in mortification, as she dropped into a deep curtsy. What a gudgeon he must think her. And close upon this thought came the realization that here was one of the infamous misogynic Inconquerables. No doubt her series of faux pas had served only to underscore his disdain of the fairer sex. And why, indeed, had he not made himself known once he had learned she was to be a fellow guest of his at Applegarth? It would have been the civil thing to do.

Suddenly her lively sense of the ridiculous came to her aid. She had certainly begun her debut into society in a highly unorthodox fashion. She little doubted that her reputation was forever ruined. Henceforth, she would be known as the female who had been so coming as to rescue the noted nonpareil in a torrential downpour. Such unbecoming behavior in a gently bred female would damn her in the eyes of polite society. Really, it was all too absurd. No doubt Tess would be more than a little put out with her protégée for her fall from grace before she had even donned her first evening gown, but disgrace mattered little as far as Miranda was concerned. After all, she had never wished to cut a dash in society. And now that her advent into the fashionable enclaves had been precluded by fate, she might as well make the best of things.

She experienced a sudden heady surge of rebelliousness. All her life she had had to tread the narrow path of duty and respectability for the sake of the children, that they might live down the feckless reputation of her rakish father and his eldest offspring. Well, now that her reputation had been tattered beyond mending and through no real fault of her own, she had little left to lose. She had come to Applegarth to enjoy herself, and that was what she meant to do. But first she must deal with the troublesome duke who had been the inadvertent cause of her downfall, and who had had the temerity to judge her wanting in proper decorum.

It was thus that, as Miranda rose from her curtsy, the duke was treated to a beguiling sparkle of laughter in the cool green eyes.

"Your Grace," she murmured in her rich contralto, "it is fortunate that at last we have been formally introduced, for it seems our fate to be forever thrust into each other's company. I can only hope that in future we shall meet under less trying circumstances."

Then, at Lady Tess's look of befuddlement, Miranda's lilting laughter bubbled forth in earnest.

"I have not behaved at ail as you would have wished, dear Tess," Miranda confessed when at last she had control of her voice again. "I fear I have forever sunk myself beneath reproach. For not only have I flung myself headlong into His Grace's arms and assaulted his person in a most grievous manner, but I have, in trying to save the duke's team from injury, gone beyond what is considered polite behavior. In

short, I am an impetuous female in need of proper
male guidance. Do you think we might find someone
willing to take on the task?'' And, compelled by a
devil she had never suspected lurked within herself, she
flashed a thoroughly roguish grin at the bemused nobleman.

Good God! He inwardly recoiled. Was this practiced flirt the graceless spinster who allegedly dis-
avowed any interest in matrimony? His first impression of her, upon being nearly bowled over at the
inn, was of an impertinent wench with a total disre-
gard for her own appearance. She had been decked out
in an impossible gown that might have done her
grandmama credit but did little to enhance the unprepossessing face unfashionably freckled and framed in
flaming hair topped by a bonnet that could be described only as an eyesore. He had judged her upon
first glance to be a provincial, and upon learning her
identity from the unwitting abigail had inwardly
groaned at being obligated to attempt to charm such
an antidote. However, a wager was a wager, and immediately he had begun his assault upon her vaunted
defenses. She had just as quickly, however, relieved
him of any illusion he might have had that she would
fall easy victim to his charm. She was no fool, was the
redoubtable spinster and he had been forced to re-
vamp his strategy.

He had not been prepared to behold her gamely
slipping and sliding through the mud and rain to come
to his aid with a resourcefulness and coolheadedness
that would have done credit to any man. For the first
time he had really looked at her as she sat shivering in

the coach, her absurd hair streaming mud and water about her face. She was no beauty, but he had been struck by something unique and fine about her uncomplaining fortitude and the solicitude she displayed for the child. She was certainly no simpering miss, for she had not been averse, despite her patent weariness, to exchanging words with him with a pertness that did her no discredit in his eyes.

Suddenly he had been ashamed of his indiscreet wager with Charles, a feeling he had seldom experienced before and one that he had found more than a little distasteful. And now she dared to turn beguiling green eyes upon him and flirt in a thoroughly outrageous manner.

The dark arrogant brows snapped together, and the heavy eyelids drooped in an expression of ennui as it occurred to him that he had been properly duped. No doubt the indomitable Miss Waincourt had planned her strategy well. Disarming him with her ridiculous disguise, she had led him to believe she was just as Charles had so obligingly described her. But, made overconfident by her apparent success in pulling the wool over his eyes, she had let slip the mask of the determined spinster to reveal the true character of the female on the hunt. She was an undisciplined hoyden who deserved to be taught a lesson. Well, he would oblige her, but not to the end she undoubtedly had had in mind. He had been hunted before.

"It would be a rare treat to have the schooling of such an enchanting female," he murmured insinuatingly, a dangerous glint in the sleepy blue eyes. "And if you mean to grant me that office, surely we can dispense with formality. My intimates call me Evan. I should be pleased were you to do the same, my dear.''

"Ah, but I cannot be numbered among those fortunate few, my lord Duke,'' the impertinent chit simpered, smiling sweetly. "Why, I should be considered quite forward, and understandably so. After all, we have only just been introduced, and who can tell whether we shall ever attain such intimacy as would permit the use of our Christian names?'' Her fluttering eyelashes would seem to promise otherwise, he noted grimly. "Somehow I do not think it a likely event,'' she added with a provocative wave of one slender, mud-soiled hand. "I have so little time for frivolity, you see.''

She did not afford him the opportunity to retort to her masterful setdown, as she swiftly curtsied. She noted only the narrowing of his gaze upon her face before she smilingly excused herself and, grabbing a dumbfounded Tess by the arm, propelled her cousin toward the stairs.

"Miranda!'' scolded that scandalized lady in a shocked whisper. "How could you snub Eversley so? The man was most gracious to count you among his friends. It was a condescension few would care to scorn.''

"That is precisely what it was, dear Tess,'' asserted the unrepentant Miranda. "Condescension! Well, duke or no duke, I will not be treated so.''

"Oh, dear. I do fear you have misjudged Evan. Really, one cannot afford to alienate him. With a single word he can make you a success or ruin you quite utterly.''

"Pooh! He can do nothing to me. In two weeks' time I shall be back at Groves and less even than a memory to the torpid duke."

In spite of her horror at her young cousin's reckless folly, Lady Tess giggled. How Evan would hate such a name. She sobered quickly, however, at the certainty that her scheme had gone awry before it had ever had a chance to unfold.

"I cannot forgive you for ruining yourself, my dear," she said with a heartfelt sigh. "When I had such high hopes of... Well, never mind. Perhaps all is not yet lost."

She ignored Miranda's quizzing look and ushered her briskly down the hall to her bedchamber. Peggy was there before them, busily unpacking Miranda's trunk. Two maids were already pouring cans of hot water into a round porcelain tub before a blazing fire.

Miranda shivered and sneezed. She was suddenly uncomfortably aware of a slight scratching sensation at the back of her throat and inwardly groaned. How could she succumb to an ague now of all times? she asked herself and meekly submitted to Peggy's help in undressing while her cousin fussed over her like a mother hen with one chick.

"You will soak for as long as you like in your bath, my dear," she said and frowned thoughtfully at the sight of Miranda's meager wardrobe. The child cannot appear in such rags, she thought to herself.

Miranda had had little time for socializing even with the rather limited opportunities in the country and had allowed her wardrobe to suffer as a result. Most of the gowns had been designed and made up for a much

younger girl. Miranda and Agatha had altered and
refurbished them as best they could in so short a time,
yet there was no mistaking their unsuitability for a
lovely woman past her first blush of youth. Tess eyed
the tall, slender figure of the younger woman consid-
eringly and mentally shook her head. Her cousin
topped her own five feet by a good nine inches. It
would take a miracle to alter any of her own gowns for
Miranda's use. Nor was the copper-colored hair suited
to the colors worn by the blond Lady Tess. Something must be done and done at once, she decided,
then fondly kissed her cousin on the cheek and wished
her a peaceful repose.

Miranda sighed with relief at finding herself suddenly alone, as the abigail, too, left to dispose of her
mistress's ruined gown properly. She sank gratefully
into the steaming bath and allowed her weary muscles
to relax. Almost she could have drifted off to sleep.
Instead, she let her thoughts wander aimlessly until she
realized they had conjured up the high cheekbones and
heavy-lidded eyes of the Duke of Eversley. Immediately the languid spell was broken.

She had certainly made a dramatic entrance into
society, she reflected ruefully and then sternly reminded herself that she had nothing of which to be
ashamed. Yet somehow she was not comforted as she
recalled sleepy eyes the color of brilliant sapphires.

"Pooh!" she exclaimed, slashing at the bathwater
with a closed fist. It was no skin off her nose if the
precious duke had taken her in dislike. She had not
come to Applegarth to court the acceptance of that
toplofty nobleman. She had come to enjoy a brief time

away from her responsibilities. She was going to have a marvelous time, she vowed, then sneezed three times in quick succession.

"Oh, dear." She sighed and sank back against the edge of the tub. "At least I cannot further disgrace myself if I am to be confined to my room with a stuffy nose." The prospect brought her to the brink of tears. But firmly chiding herself for a silly peagoose, she called the abigail to wash her hair. Sometime later, she was snugly curled up in the huge four-poster bed, a stack of handkerchiefs near to hand.

CHAPTER FOUR

MIRANDA SLEPT FITFULLY through the night and awoke with puffy eyes and a red nose. Sunlight streamed through the lace curtains, denoting mid-morning. A bouquet of freshly cut wildflowers stood in a Sèvres vase on a bedside table: fragrant honey-suckle intermingled with pink rosebuds and blue for-get-me-nots. Wistfully she sniffed the blossoms, only to fall into a fit of sneezing.

"Oh, I might as well pack up and go home," she moaned aloud when the paroxysm had passed.

"Nonsense," said her cousin as she breezed into the room. "I have waited an age for this visit and shall not give you up so easily." Lady Tess halted beside the bed and looked compassionately down at the miserable girl. "We shall put your period of confinement to good use. Really, Miranda, how could you let your wardrobe go to such rack and ruin? You are not a pauper. Do you never see anyone at Groves? These will never do, you know," she added, going to the clothespress and drawing out several of the out-moded, girlish gowns.

Miranda smiled wanly at the delectable picture of her petite cousin gowned in a pale rose sarcenet round gown, the skirt of which fell in straight lines from an

Empire waist just below her rounded bosom and was gathered in loose folds at the low V in back. The sleeves were puffed over the shoulders, then conformed tightly to the arms, ending in embroidered rosebuds over the back of the hands *à la Mamelouk*. Her tiny feet were shod in matching pale rose bottines with silk ribbons threaded across the fronts. Her pale blond hair was swept atop her head and allowed to cascade down the back of her head in a profusion of loose curls. She looked as if she had just stepped form the pages of *La Belle Assemblée*, Miranda thought wistfully.

Miranda had never been one to consider her own appearance overmuch. If she thought about it at all, it was to judge herself too tall, too thin and much too busy to be concerned over it. Her red hair was naturally curly, an attribute that might have been the envy of many a female who spent each night in curling papers or hours wrestling with a curling iron, had it not been curly to excess. It frizzed in a flaming cloud about her face and over her shoulders. No amount of diligence on her part could tame the wild mane into a semblance of Grecian curls or create even an illusion of *la Méduse*. She wore it for the most part in braids wrapped about her head or tied it back with a riband at the nape of her neck. Furthermore, her creamy, translucent skin, so characteristic of true redheads, showed a lamentable tendency to freckle. Only her eyes laid any real claim to beauty, and even they were exceptions to the classic mode. Of a deep emerald green and lavishly fringed in dark lashes, they were, nonetheless, decidedly slanted upward, giving her countenance a rather exotic cast. Her nose was short and straight, her mouth full and inclined to quirk humorously. A single dimple lurked alluringly at the left corner of her mouth whenever she smiled. All in all, she presented a picture of enchanting mischief, which, had she known it, was far more beguiling than mere beauty.

Lady Tess, regarding her with arms folded across her bosom and the slim forefinger of one hand pressed against pursed lips, was not unaware of this. In truth, she intended to take full advantage of it. Her gaze fell on the bouquet of wildflowers, and a curious glimmer sparked in the blue depths.

"Oh, how lovely!" she cried in innocent rapture. "Now, whoever can they be from?"

Miranda awarded her cousin a faintly surprised glance out of watery eyes. "I assumed they were due to your thoughtfulness," she said with a shrug.

"Well, I did not send them up. Is there a card? Oh, yes. Here it is." Her nimble fingers withdrew an ivory calling card bearing the Eversley crest. Disregarding her cousin's fluttering hand, she turned the card over and perused the brief message scrawled in a bold hand across the back.

"It seems our brief encounters heretofore must be cursed with mischance. May I hope you will condescend to try a third? They do say it is the charm."

It was signed simply *E.W.*

Miranda pretended a nonchalance she was far from feeling. She was, in fact, prey to a variety of conflicting emotions, chief of which was a feeling that she had, perhaps, misjudged the gentleman. It naturally followed that she had behaved rather badly. Certainly she must apologize. Yet how difficult it would be to humble herself before the arrogant nobleman. Adding to her confusion and chagrin was a delicious sensation of anticipation that warred with a demoralizing feeling of dread. How could she face him again? She strove not to squirm beneath the interested scrutiny of her cousin and experienced a distant sensation of foreboding at the unnatural gleam in Lady Tess's blue eyes.

"Well, well, well," mused the lady enigmatically. "The sleeping cat stirs."

"I beg your pardon?"

"Nothing, my dear," Tess answered briefly. "But now we must get to work. There is much to be done and little time in which to do it."

Miranda regarded her petite cousin in bewilderment. "Do what?"

"Why, spruce up your image, of course," she replied, scrutinizing her cousin as though Miranda were a piece of clay waiting to be sculpted.

"Why ever should I want to do that?" Miranda asked suspiciously.

"Does not every woman wish to look her best?" Tess countered with profound innocence. "Besides, you could not come to me when I wished to bring you out, and I had so looked forward to it. You must allow me this small pleasure, Miranda. I have summoned the local dressmaker. She is a genius with a needle. We shall whip up just a few things while you recover from this most unfortunate malady."

"You, my dearest cousin, are up to your old matchmaking tricks again. I know you."

"Miranda, I'm sure I do not know what you are talking about," Tess replied with an injured air. "I simply thought to brighten your convalescence. Please humor me in this. It would make me very happy."

Miranda studied the pleading face of her cousin. It could be true, after all, that Tess sought only to alleviate the onset of boredom in the country.

"Are you sure you are not playing a matchmaking game?" Miranda persisted, though she had softened perceptibly. "You seemed, for instance, uncommonly put out to think the duke had taken me in dislike."

"The duke?" queried Tess on a trill of laughter. "La, child, one does not think in such terms of Eversley. I wrote to you, did I not, that he is a confirmed bachelor and a rake. Much as I love you, my dearest Miranda, I do not delude myself that you could capture his interest. You are simply not in his style. He prefers, I fear, barques of frailty to young women of quality. An early, ill-judged tendre that turned out badly has hardened his heart irrevocably against matrimony. Believe me when I tell you, I seek only to please myself by transforming you into a young lady of fashion. Please say you will allow me to do it."

"You are a complete hand, Tess," Miranda said and grinned at her cousin's conniving. She would be boorish in the extreme if she refused such kindhearted generosity. But she sobered quickly as a new thought occurred to her.

Miranda did not like to admit to the older woman that she could ill afford the expense of a new wardrobe. Already she had kept the younger boys out of school longer than she liked in the hope that Groves might soon be better able to support the expenditure. Then, too, there was the salary of the new governess to consider, and the new stud she had been angling to buy for the brood mares. If only she had her competence now, she thought with a sigh. But the inheritance was held in trust until her twenty-fifth birthday or until she should marry, whichever came first. Ruefully she smiled at her cousin and shook her head.

"You know I would do anything for you, Tess," she said and blew her nose. "But truth to tell, I have not the funds for such folderols. And no, do not say you will oblige me. I cannot accept charity."

"But your competence..."

"Will not be released to me until I am five and twenty."

"Miranda, do not be such a peagoose. I shall simply advance you the necessary funds until then. Consider it an investment. There's no use arguing. You know I cannot be denied once I have set my mind to a thing. And I promise we shall purchase only a few things. After all, it is not as if you are to be presented at court. Now, don't you worry about it. Madame Tusseaud will arrive directly and we shall begin. Oh, it will be such fun! I fear I have grown quite dull of late. You are a godsend, my dear."

MIRANDA FOUND HERSELF swept along in a whirlwind of planning. First she must have her hair cut and styled, then a cucumber lotion must be applied to fade the offending freckles. Spenser, Tess's own lady's maid, who possessed an uncanny gift with hair, was summoned. She stood for a long time scrutinizing Miranda from every angle. She brushed out the thick mane of frizzy, coppery waves and furrowed her brow in serious thought.

"It is hopeless, I know," Miranda remarked sympathetically. "I have never been able to do a thing with it."

"Oh, no, my lady," said the woman in manifest surprise. "You have beautiful hair. 'Tis only lacking the right cut." And she set to with scissors and comb. In no time Miranda's long hair lay in piles upon the floor. The abigail gave a last swipe with the comb, then stepped back to view her handiwork.

Miranda gaped in admiration at her reflection in the looking glass. Spenser had cut her tresses in two-inch lengths all over her head, then swept the curls outward from the crown. Freed from the weight of the long, thick mass, her hair bounced in soft, alluring curls. The fuller style softened the prominent cheekbones, making Miranda's face appear rounder and less long.

Miranda thought she had never looked so well, but the abigail was not satisfied. She vigorously applied cucumber cream to Miranda's freckles and made her promise to repeat the treatment three times a day. Nor must she venture out without bonnet and sunshade, "else all would have been for naught."

Miranda suffered these ministrations stoically, secretly amused by the serious conferences between mistress and abigail concerning cosmetics and lotions. They resembled staff officers planning battle strategy, she thought, then wondered uncomfortably just what battle Tess had in mind for her. She was not given time to ponder seriously the game her cousin played before she was firmly launched into phase two of the battle plan.

The seamstress, a French émigrée, was a middle-aged widow with shrewd Gallic eyes. There was a briskness about her every movement that gave the impression that she was never idle. She listened to her employer's instructions, her glittering black eyes never straying from Miranda's face and figure.

"You wish the wardrobe *utilitaire? Oui. Je comprends bien.* It is not *difficile. Mademoiselle* suits *bien* the mode. So tall and slender she is! You will see how we make the few gowns appear like many. Now, you will stand very still, *oui?* And we will take the measurements."

Somehow Miranda, despite an aching head, a touch of fever, and a perpetually runny nose, got through the endless morning of fittings. She could not understand how anyone could derive pleasure from being tortured by pins and hours of standing at attention while fabrics were held up to her and patterns were fitted to her protesting body. She had to choose from among a multitude of samples—muslins, poplins, printed cottons, satins, jaconet, lutestring and crepe. Her head was fairly awhirl with indecision about all but the color, which Madame Tusseaud insisted could be nothing but shades of green, ivory or russet. "Anything else would be to war with *Mademoiselle*'s unique coloring,'' the seamstress insisted with a vehement gesture of her expressive hands.

Miranda grew weary long before the last pattern was decided upon. She had seen pictures of round gowns with gathered flounces or scalloped hems, debated the merits of frocks with high stomachers versus low stomachers, sighed obediently over zephyr shifts with overtunics of Valenciennes lace or barege, rejected with a horrified giggle a Grecian robe slit up the sides to reveal shapely legs clear to the thighs. But at last the decisions were made, and she was allowed a meager luncheon of chicken broth, dry toast and weak tea before being confined to her bed for a long beauty rest.

She was awakened late in the afternoon to a second treatment of cucumber lotion and Cook's bitter tisane. Spenser shook her head and clicked her tongue reprovingly at the sight of Miranda's split and uneven fingernails. She soaked the young lady's hands in a softening mixture scented with strawberries, until the skin of her hands shriveled in protest. Then her nails were shaped and polished while Miranda nodded off.

That evening a second bouquet of wildflowers was delivered to her door. The dressing bell had rung sometime earlier, as Sir Charles preferred to keep country hours, and Miranda, sitting propped up in her bed, wrapped in a kerseymere shawl, was wistfully envisioning the bounteous meal to which the others would soon be summoned. The soft scratching on her door heralded the arrival of the scanty repast thought suitable to a convalescent. A maid entered bearing a bed tray resplendent with forget-me-nots and Miranda's rather less impressive supper of soft-boiled eggs, dry toast and tea.

Miranda experienced an odd fluttering of her heart at the sight of the card bearing a familiar bold hand.

"Tarry not overlong in your tower," she read, her cheeks flaming. "I grow impatient to teach you my name."

"What fustian!" she proclaimed with a gurgle of laughter to the empty room and tenderly tucked the absurd card with its predecessor beneath her pillow.

She felt utterly foolish for so sentimental a gesture, which had hitherto not been a part of her nature, and almost succumbed to the less romantical impulse to fling the silly things into the fire. For she seemed constantly and maddeningly aware of their presence, as though they were phantoms lurking beneath her pillow solely to torment her with ridiculous fantasies. In the end, she was become quite miserable.

"It is only this absurd cold," she told herself and sipped halfheartedly at her tepid tea. That and Tess's apparent determination to starve her into submission, she reflected wryly as she poked at the offending eggs with her fork.

When she had finished with the tray, she rang to have it removed, then prepared to pass the night as best she could after having slept the afternoon away. It seemed as if her bed had been suddenly transformed into a medieval torture rack. She tossed and turned, trying to discover a position that would ease the persistent ache of muscles unaccustomed to long periods abed, until finally she gave up the effort altogether.

Impatiently she thrust aside the bedclothes and climbed down from the high poster bed. It occurred to her that a book might lull her to sleep, so she straightened the muslin cap that hid her bright curls and slipped a dressing gown over her cotton nightdress. Then she stood uncertainly in the center of her room, as her bare toes curled into the thick woolen carpet reminded her that she was without her slippers, which had suffered the same fate as Mistress Charity Graves's figwort. It would be highly improper for her to venture forth in bare feet, and yet she was reluctant to give up the notion of slipping to the book room in exchange for hours of sleepless torture. Surely she ran little risk of being caught, she told herself, since Tess and Charles were wont to keep early hours in the country. In moments she was slipping noiselessly down the long hall, a hand cupped about the flame of a candle to keep it from going out.

It was close to midnight, she saw as she passed an oakwood case clock. She breathed a sigh of relief. No doubt the company would be dispersed to their various rooms. She had no desire to be discovered roaming the halls barefoot and in her nightclothes. She glided down the sweeping staircase to the ground floor and opened several doors off the hall before discovering the library.

The book room was spacious, with rows of glassed shelves lining the walls ceiling high on three sides. The fourth wall housed a gothic fireplace, the carved stone gleaming eerily in the red glow of a low-burning fire. Twin love seats faced each other across a low, clawed-foot mahogany table. Tall-backed chairs covered in red damask fronted the fireplace. Absently Miranda twirled a huge globe set in an oak stand near a partner's desk with ormolu handles gleaming in the candlelight. The low rumble sounded loud in the hush of the sleeping house. A chill crept down her back beneath the fabric of her nightdress. She was tiptoeing across the claret-colored Ushak rug toward the fire when a movement from one of the wing chairs froze her into immobility. Breathlessly she watched a long, lean figure unfold itself from one of the chairs.

"Ah, Miss Waincourt," said a deep baritone rich with amusement. "I had not hoped you would seek me out so swiftly. I am pleasantly surprised."

CHAPTER FIVE

MIRANDA GREW RIGID with embarrassment. Despite
the fact that her rather bulky cotton dressing gown,
made up on the lines of practicality for warmth rather
than style, as chastely concealed her slender form as
did her shapeless woolen day dresses, she was acutely
aware of the impropriety of being alone with a gentleman in such dishabille. One slim hand unconsciously
clutched the front of her gown, while she curled her
bare toes under in a futile attempt to conceal them
beneath the hem. She hoped the red glow of the fire
disguised her crimson cheeks as she lifted her head to
stare into the darkly shadowed face of the Duke of
Eversley.

She wondered if she was cursed to find herself forever at a disadvantage when she met this man, as she
took in the double-breasted corbeau cutaway coat and
light serge-green breeches, which appeared molded to
muscular thighs. Patent leather pumps with diamond
buckles, silk clock-worked stockings, and an immaculate neckcloth arranged in the Oriental all proclaimed the town beau in elegant evening wear.
Petulantly she judged him overdressed for the country, but unaccountably could not still the sudden racing of her heart. Inwardly she chided herself for a

ninnyhammer. Why had she not remained within the safety of her room? Well, there was no turning back now. She was properly caught, and it behooved her to get herself out of this new coil with what remained of her tattered dignity.

"I beg your pardon," she said with as much composure as she could, "if I have led you to believe I am remotely desirous of a clandestine meeting with Your Grace. I was merely seeking a cure for insomnia. I thought perhaps a book . . . But I have no wish to disturb your solitude. I beg you will excuse me."

She turned and strode regally toward the door, her back held perfectly straight. It was a proud exit, worthy of applause, she thought, then blushed furiously as the effect was spoiled by an ominous growl in her stomach. She was brought to an abrupt halt by the duke's low chuckle.

"It would seem that your unwelcome vigil would be best cured not by the devouring of a weighty tome but by the ingestion of a substantial meal. Mayhap I can be of some service, ma'am. It happens I am well acquainted with the nether regions of Applegarth and can find my way with ease to the kitchens." When she hesitated, he took a step toward her. "Cannot we cry pax for the time being, child?" he asked softly. "After all, I should not be able to sleep myself knowing you to be near to swooning with hunger."

He was taken aback as he saw her slender shoulders begin to tremble. Egad, what had he said to overset her so? She had not seemed the missish sort to succumb to tears of embarrassment. He reached out a shapely hand to turn her around and was treated to an impish countenance convulsed in mirth. Her gurgle of laughter brought a bemused smile to his finely chiseled lips. He watched her slim hand rise to her lips to stifle her laughter, but not before he had glimpsed an enchanting dimple peep out at the corner of her mouth.

"I—I beg your pardon, Your Grace," she gasped as her giggles finally subsided. Her slanted eyes with the dark, sweeping lashes held him captive. "It is too absurd that every time we have met, I seem cursed to play the fool. You must think me an utter gudgeon. And who can blame you? Yet I assure you I am considered a sensible female of unexceptional manners. I cannot think what whimsy of fate persists in sinking me beneath reproach."

"Not beneath reproach, surely," he said with an answering gleam of amusement in his eye. "Aside from taking undue risks to aid a fellow traveler, a rather unnerving disposition to ward off violently the innocent advances of unwelcome strangers, and a deuced hasty temper that leads you to misjudge overtures of gratitude, one could find little for which to reproach you. On the contrary, I am grateful to have met one who must be termed an original."

"Oh." She choked back a bubble of laughter. "You are incorrigible. How ungallant to remind me of my faux pas when I have so graciously apologized. It is too bad of you."

"Indubitably. I see I must make reparation. I shall presently wine and dine you. But first, pray be seated before the fire. For a sensible female you seem uncommonly bent on courting a fatal inflammation of the lungs. What possessed you to go wandering about in bare feet?"

"It is the most vexatious thing," she replied ingenuously, "but when I went to pack my slippers in my trunk, I could find only the shredded remains of one shoe. I have no doubt that the reprehensible Hannibal had taken them for his supper. He possesses an iron stomach and is totally lacking in discrimination. He will eat anything, a trait that has had disastrous results in the past and will, I've no doubt, bring us all to grief in the end."

"Hannibal, I trust, is not a *close* relation?" observed the duke mildly, with only a slight twitch at the corners of his mouth. "He sounds a boorish fellow one would not gladly welcome into one's household. A distant cousin, perhaps, whom you have taken in out of civility and cannot now persuade to leave?"

"Oh, no," Miranda cried, giggling at such an absurdity. "Hannibal is a goat for whom my young sister Allie has developed a decided tendre. I have forbidden him the run of the house, but she will sneak him in when no one is attending. And I have not the heart to put him away, though he is like to deprive me of my sanity, for he has been good for her. She has been a sickly child and only lately has begun to gain in health, thanks, I must own, to her attachment to Hannibal."

The duke, observing a sudden alteration in his companion's mood evidenced by a slight furrow in the smooth brow, was quick to divert Miranda's thoughts from Allie and the troublesome Hannibal. Taking the candle from her hand, he firmly grasped her by the elbow to lead her to the recently vacated wing chair. There he covered her with a decorative shawl that had been draped over the back of one of the love seats.

"Now," he said as he straightened and stood eyeing her from his considerable height, "promise me you will not vanish while I am gone. I shan't be long."

Before she could answer, he made her a courtly bow and, taking the candle with him, left to forage for food in the kitchens. She watched his broad back retreat across the library. He moved with a slow, catlike grace, she thought and was suddenly reminded of Lady Tess's puzzling remark concerning sleeping cats. An uncomfortable suspicion took root in her mind. But no, she told herself firmly, her cousin had made it quite clear she did not consider Miranda of sufficient wit or beauty to engage the interest of the Duke of Eversley, nor did she herself believe it to be feasible. She was, after all, a tall, plain girl with little to attract such a nonpareil. No. She had nothing to fear in that quarter.

Somehow the thought did not comfort her. She attributed the sudden hollow feeling in her stomach to hunger and firmly turned her thoughts from the torpid duke to thoughts of her beloved Groves. But as contemplation of the possible catastrophic events that might be occurring at home brought her even less peace of mind, she was grateful for the eventual return of the duke bearing a tray laden with cold victuals.

Her delicious giggle sounded anew at sight of the elegantly clad nobleman bowing before her, a white linen towel draped over one arm in the manner of a serving man. The hooded eyes glinted with reflected amusement, and Miranda was suddenly acutely aware of the easy charm and unquestionable magnetism of the man.

"Dinner is served, my lady," he drawled in the affected tones of a proper English butler, as he proffered pigeon pie, slices of roast beef, a baked fowl, tangy cheese, sweetmeats and wine.

"You have outdone yourself, my lord Duke," Miranda said, her voice vibrant with amusement. "I do hope you mean to join me. I cannot possibly eat all of this."

"No, I did not suppose you could. I confess I was hoping for your invitation."

He settled himself comfortably in the second wing chair and helped himself to a sizeable portion of the repast.

Gradually Miranda was disarmed by her companion's ease of manner. He entertained her with *on dits* of the beau monde with a keen wit that was never cruel or mean. She was fascinated by tales of elaborate balls in vast ballrooms decorated with bolts of silk suspended from the ceilings to create an illusion of diaphanous clouds or transformed into gardens with potted plants, even trees resplendent with birds in gilded cages, ranged about the dance floor. She blushed at the description of ladies in flimsy gowns, their skirts dampened so that they clung provocatively, of painted toenails and rings worn on the ladies' toes. She giggled at the image of dandies in cossacks gathered at the ankles and neckcloths wrapped so thickly about the neck that the chin rested in them. It was a world foreign to her workaday existence, one that both fascinated and repelled.

Miranda learned that the duke was one of the Carlton set, intimates of the Prince Regent, who had a reputation for high flying. She had heard even in the isolation of Groves of Prinny's exorbitant entertainments. Accounts of sumptuous repasts served on vast tables down which an artificial stream had been made to flow with goldfish swimming before one's dinner plate vied with reports of fortunes spent on the furnishing of the Prince Regent's Marine Palace at Brighton. Prinny's mistresses and numerous by-blows were common knowledge, and she was not hard put to imagine this handsome, soft-spoken nobleman as one of the Regent's intimates. No doubt that accounted for the cynicism that enveloped him like a protective cloak, and the torpidity for which he was renowned and which seemed in abeyance then in the soft glow of the firelight over the impromptu picnic in the bookroom at Applegarth.

The duke's blue eyes shimmered with lively humor. The lazy smile, usually little more than a cynical twist of the lips, had broadened into an engaging grin. His rich chuckle brought a warm glow to Miranda's cheeks, and she found herself liking this unaffected man.

With a disarming subtlety, he led her into revealing much of herself, and she found herself describing her beloved Groves, the children and her dear Aunt Agatha.

"I suppose some would account us an eccentric lot, and indeed, it is not usual these days to encounter an elderly lady in wide hoops, heavy brocades and a beak-brimmed bonnet a good two and a half feet high. But Aunt Agatha is a dear. She would do anything for any one of us.''

All at once she grew aware that she had been speaking at great length of matters that could not possibly concern the urbane duke. Self-consciously she turned abashed eyes on her companion.

"I beg your pardon, my lord Duke," she said with a becoming blush. "I do not usually prose on so about domestic matters.''

"Now you have done it," he accused and shook his head dolefully.

A quizzical smile curved Miranda's lips.

"Your Grace?" she said.

"For the past hour we have been conversing quite pleasantly as two equals. Why now must you suddenly recall my title? Can you not bring yourself to use my given name? If you dislike Evan, there are several others to choose from, among them George, William and Fredrick. Or at the least you can call me Eversley. It is not a difficult name to pronounce, unless, of course, you are French and find the *r* beyond your capability. You are not, are you, French?''

"My lord, you are being absurd. You know I am not," she answered with a low chuckle.

"No? Excellent. Then we shall have no more of your lord dukes or Your Graces. And as for prosing on about domestic matters, you may have my leave to do so at any time. I shall be the judge of whether or not you bore me. Contrary to your fears, I have seldom been so well entertained. Your family sounds both charming and unusual. But tell me: do you never indulge yourself?''

Miranda blinked in surprise at the question. He had taken her off guard, and she answered promptly without thinking.

"I have little time for self-indulgence. Yet I am not discontent. I have the satisfaction of seeing the children and Groves grow daily more self-reliant. I am needed there.''

"And when you are no longer needed? What then?''

"But I shall always be needed, Your Grace.'' She laughed and shook her head at his grimace of displeasure. "The children will one day marry and have children of their own. No doubt they will have need of me.''

"What utter absurdity!'' he said and leaned forward the better to see her face. "You cannot mean to degenerate into a prim and proper aunt. And all in the name of duty, no doubt. Egad, child, have you no awareness of yourself? What an utter waste you plan to make of your life. And I deplore waste.''

"Do you, my lord?'' Miranda queried ironically, wondering how they came suddenly to be at loggerheads but unable to stop her wayward tongue. "I feel sure you are a proper judge of such matters. You are, after all, a duke.''

"Oh, you are quite right to censure me,'' he said with an appreciative gleam in his eye at her masterly setdown. "I am, after all, a frippery fellow, am I not? But it is not I who claim selfless devotion to be a quality to be admired. Such bloodless self-sacrifice is better suited to the missionary. Are you of the religious persuasion, Miss Waincourt? Are your few moments of leisure devoted to charitable works?''

"How curious that you should be intolerant of all the virtues held in esteem by civilized peoples," she retorted, her chin going up. "A self-confessed idler famous for his indolence and proud of his affiliation with the Carlton set. From what profundity of thought can you judge duty to one's family or the self-satisfaction of having reared three children? You, an adamant bachelor?''

"Oh, bravo," applauded the duke with a cynical curl of his lips. "You have given me my own, no doubt. And yet I wonder how such an advocate of home and family can condemn herself to so barren a role as aunt.''

"And what would you have me to do, my lord?" she countered bitterly, goaded by his intolerance to an unwise justification of the role that had been thrust upon her through no fault of her own. "Throw my cap at the nearest unattached man who comes my way that I might enjoy the lauded fulfillment of marriage? That is the proper province of woman, is it not? To submit in marriage to a man, any man willing to offer her the protection of his precious name. And in exchange, to bow to his authority, to gratify his every wish, to relinquish her independent thought, her fortune, and her autonomy to his rule, whether or no he is worthy of such trust. Well, I am fortunate to have experienced the fulfillment of home and family without the added burden of a husband. I do not see that a wedded state would suit me better.''

"Do you not?" he drawled, a strange light in his remarkable eyes. "And yet it occurs to me that you, in your innocence, have overlooked something. I speak from experience, which tells me that there is that between a man and a woman which your boasted sterile sense of duty can never provide—needs that can only go unsatisfied in your chosen role of maiden aunt."

"Beware, my lord Duke. You go beyond the limits of what is acceptable," Miranda said, her bosom heaving in indignation. Her fingers curled around the curved claws of the armrests till the knuckles shone white.

"Then I must surely beg pardon...or follow your own example of self-sacrifice."

Miranda drew back in alarm from the sudden gleam of purpose in the gaze he bent upon her. But she was slow to judge his full intent. Before she could escape the actions of an obvious bedlamite, he had yanked her to her feet and crushed her to his hard chest. The errant thought came to her that she was experiencing déjà vu, as she once again inhaled at exceedingly close range the heady scent of shaving soap mingled with tobacco. She stood rigid and stared in horrified fascination as his mocking face drew near her own.

The kiss was surprisingly gentle and left her feeling rather dazed. He chuckled softly as he raised his head to behold her emerald eyes distant and dreamy. She looked like a bewildered child with her ridiculous muslin cap askew, allowing a coppery curl to fall across her forehead.

So long did she stare blindly into his face that he began to grow alarmed. He cursed himself for a brute to so assault her innocence, even as he experienced an odd exultation at having awakened her to a sense of herself. For at the last she had responded ever so slightly, and a small sigh had escaped her lips as he drew away. He had acted on impulse, merely thinking to teach her a lesson for her impertinence. He had not expected to feel shaken to the core by her response. Her low, whimsical utterance startled him.

"You will probably catch my cold, you know," she said gravely, a thoughtful frown upon her brow. "And it would serve you right. You have treated me quite shabbily."

"Indubitably," he responded with a chuckle. "Must I beg your pardon?"

"You should, perhaps, were I not to blame for what happened."

The sleepy eyes grew suddenly alert, but Miranda, lost in the turmoil of her own newly aroused sensations and a growing feeling of guilt at the impropriety of her attire and her position in the arms of an infamous rake, did not see the tightening of his lips or the sudden leap of the muscle along his jawline.

"I see," he remarked in a colorless voice. "Then my first suspicions were correct. You did set out to entrap a duke."

Miranda blinked in confusion. "I—I beg your pardon?"

"No need to put on missish airs with me, Miss Waincourt. Indeed, I must congratulate you on a superb campaign. Egad, to think I should fall to the scheming of a provincial without polish or countenance. You had me totally fooled. You are properly compromised beyond a doubt, as you well intended. All you need to do is cry for help. But that will not be necessary. Oh, you need not fear I shall not pay the piper. I am not in the habit of ruining innocent young maids, no matter how much they might deserve it. We shall be wed by special license three days hence.''

CHAPTER SIX

MIRANDA GASPED and, abruptly placing both hands on Eversley's offending chest, shoved with all her might. His Grace, caught off balance, toppled backward into the wing chair, nearly sending the tray bearing the leavings of their repast toppling. Only the duke's lightning reflexes saved the Ushak rug from certain ruination. He stared up, then, into the flushed face of an avenging angel. The lips that had succumbed so sweetly to his kiss trembled now in fury. The exotic eyes sparkled dangerously. Past experience with the red-haired termagant had taught him caution. He twisted aside from her savage kick, then threw back his head in a hearty laugh as she squealed and, hopping on one leg grabbed at her injured foot, which had made contact with his chair.

"Oh, you beast!" she cried, then seemed to recall herself. In belated dignity she set her injured member gingerly down and straightened. Clenched fists propped on hips and pointed chin lifted in haughty disdain, she waited for his laughter to cease, her emerald eyes flashing sparks of searing contempt.

When his convulsions had at last subsided, she smiled icily and spoke in dulcet tones.

"I am no doubt honored by your very generous offer, Your Grace. But were you the last man on earth and I at my last prayers, I would not wed you. Entrap a duke, indeed! I would rather marry the meanest beggar, the most despicable deceiver, the most decrepit roué in the realm than marry you. Indeed, I should prefer never to marry at all, which has ever been my intent. Now, at the risk of appearing uncivil, I take my leave of you in the hope that I shall never have to set eyes on you again."

She spun around on her uninjured foot and limped proudly from the room. Bitter tears of humiliation stung her eyelids, but she blinked them back, determined that she would not succumb to a fit of the vapors.

She had forgotten her candle in the heat of the moment and had to grope her way up the curving staircase and down the long hall. But at last she found her room and climbed wearily into her bed. She pounded in frustration at her inoffensive pillows, then sank down into their softness to toss and turn, her cheeks hot and flushed as though the fever had returned. At last she settled dismally on her back and contemplated her latest folly.

Clearly she was out of her depth in this cynical world of which she had once longed to be a part. Her cloistered life at Groves had hardly prepared her to meet with aplomb the unsavory advances of a practiced rake. Oh, but he was abominable! How she would like to mete out a just punishment for his insult to her. Boiled oil and finger screws were too mild for the odious Duke of Eversley. He should be humbled and humiliated, his insufferable arrogance dealt a mortal blow. For the first time in her three and twenty years she wished to have the beauty of an Aphrodite, the charms of a Circe, and the cunning of a Machiavelli. Thus did her fancy play with sweet dreams of revenge until at last sleep overcame her, an hour before daybreak.

It seemed she had hardly sunk into a deep repose before Peggy entered bearing her mistress's morning chocolate and a cheerful face that only exacerbated Miranda's foul temper. She groaned and buried her face in her pillow, determined to ignore the unwelcome harbinger of a new day.

It was not to be. No sooner had she grudgingly thanked the abigail and dismissed her than Spenser entered with a businesslike air and the cucumber concoction for miss's face. Miranda's disposition was not improved by the dresser's exclamation of dismay over the unbecoming shadows beneath Miranda's eyes.

"Whatever can you have been about, miss," cried her cousin's abigail, hands on hips. "'Tis difficult enough t' fade th' spots from off your face without I must see to your beauty rest as well."

"I am sorry, Spenser," Miranda retorted dryly. "I am sure no one can blame you for my sorry state."

Grudgingly the abigail accepted the rather dubious apology and vigorously applied the preparation until Miranda began to suspect that the disgruntled lady's maid intended banishing the unsightly blemishes by removing the outer layer of skin.

When finally the treatment was finished, Miranda studied her translucent complexion critically. It did seem the offending freckles had faded, but whether from the efficacy of cucumbers or from her confinement within doors she could not have said. She was grateful only to be left at last to a hot bath despite the dire warning that Madame Tusseaud would arrive later in the morning with the first of her new gowns.

She was to be allowed downstairs later that afternoon for tea, an event that she was quite sure was meant to be a treat. That she viewed it otherwise—in fact, that she would liefer pack her things and flee ignominiously to Groves—she dared not reveal to her well-meaning cousin, at least not without offering a plausible explanation. Since she could not tell Lady Tess the truth without compromising her reputation, there was little she could do but pray that a missive might arrive from Groves demanding her immediate return. After all, considering the potential for catastrophe contained in the characters of her abandoned loved ones, it was not at all unlikely that just such a message would arrive directly. It was not long before Miranda had convinced herself that indeed she would be saved from the dubious pleasure of having to meet the Duke of Eversley face to face over tea. Thus she greeted Madame Tusseaud with a calm she had been far from feeling upon being brutally dragged from the illusory comfort of sleep earlier that morning.

It was obvious that the seamstress was a miracle worker, for she had, not one gown, but two completed for Miranda's approval. The first was an evening dress of deceptive simplicity. Fine ivory lutestring was gathered above the waist to fall from a square décolletage to the ankle. A train flowed gracefully at the back, while short sleeves with embroidered bands complimented her slim, bare arms. The gown was without further adornment and bespoke a quiet elegance in its every line.

The second was an emerald-green jaconet frock, the bodice *à l'enfant*, with a rounded décolletage held in place by a running string *en coulisse*. The skirt was narrow and flounced along the hemline in a lighter, contrasting shade of green. Tiny ruffed sleeves left Miranda's arms bare. It was a lovely creation that accentuated Miranda's green eyes and ivory skin. Madame Tusseaud stood back with a satisfied air.

"Ah. C'est magnifique, mademoiselle. Vous êtes très jolie, oui?"

Miranda stared in awe at the tall, elegant young woman in the cheval glass. No longer did she seem all arms and legs. The gown becomingly drew attention to her hitherto hidden feminine curves. The slender column of her neck held her head proudly. The slanted green eyes glowed with the wonder of it all. Suddenly the image of sleepy blue eyes and a mocking smile intruded into her thoughts, and a becoming tinge of color touched her cheeks.

"Did I not tell you!" cried Lady Tess behind her, clapping her hands together in an expression of glee. "You, Miranda, are a diamond of the first water. And you have worked wonders, Madame Tusseaud. The next item of importance is a riding habit. My cousin will be anxious to ride, I've no doubt, and well she should, for there is no one who looks more elegant on horseback. And after that, a walking dress, another evening gown, a morning gown, and, last, a ball gown. Can you do it?''

"*Mais oui, madame.* I have taken on the assistants who even now work on the habit. You shall have it tomorrow afternoon, I think. And I myself will undertake the walking dress. *Oui.* We will do it.''

"Excellent!'' Tess approved.

When the seamstress had gathered her things and left, Lady Tess grabbed Miranda's hands and danced her merrily around the room.

"Oh, it will be such great sport setting the Three Inconquerables on their heels,'' she exulted, all caution thrown to the wind in her exuberance. "I vow they haven't a prayer.''

The two ladies collapsed giggling upon the damask-covered settee. Miranda gasped for breath even as she fixed her cousin with an intent gaze.

"Tell me about these Three Inconquerables, Tess,'' she said. "Who are they and why are you so set against them?''

"Set against them, my dear?'' Tess echoed incredulously. "Indeed, I should never be any such thing. I am prodigiously fond of them all. And that is why I have determined to teach them the folly of their ways.''

Lady Tess grinned impishly. Her eyes sparkled with twin devils of mischief, and Miranda felt a growing alarm. How well she knew that look!

"Surely you have heard of the three most determined, most eminently eligible bachelors in the realm?'' her cousin said conspiratorially. "Lord Harkness, Earl of Chomney; Lord Bannington, Marquess of Pulvney; and Evan Westlake, Duke of

Eversley. They have taken oaths never to marry, and they stick together in their resolve, like patriots facing an overwhelming enemy. You know how stubborn men become when they feel their honor is at stake. They would rather die than suffer loss of honor. They have even made Charles swear never to aid in any plot to entrap them. And this because I merely suggested once that Heloise Dorrington would make one of them a fine wife.''

Miranda coughed gently and cocked a disbelieving eyebrow at her cousin. Tess bristled slightly in pretended indignation, then threw up her hands in a gesture of submission, her gurgle of laughter rippling through the room.

"Well, perhaps I did seek to bring Pulvney and her together at Caroline Hefton's house party a few years ago. But 'twas nothing to signify. Heloise fell straightaway for Lord Perry Esterbrook, though how she could prefer that young jackanapes to a man of polish like Jeremy, I'm sure I could not say. At any rate, the scheme came to naught, and Charles has sworn never to abet me in another. So you see, I am quite at *point non plus*."

"Tess . . ." Miranda prodded in a stern voice.

"Well, I am, dear Miranda,'' Tess said at her most beguiling. "You might have succeeded in snaring one of them. But I know you have no interest in entering the wedded state. You are far too busy taking on all your brother's responsibilities to consider matrimony. And what need have you for a man, after all? You are not like the rest of our sex. You are independent, self-sufficient, educated like a man. You are far too strong ever to need the support of a husband. How I envy you."

Miranda looked incredulously at her cousin's sweet countenance. Lady Tess wore a sad mien totally devoid of its customary mischief. Now whatever was her irrepressible cousin up to this time? she wondered, but could detect no hint of deviousness in the clear gaze lifted to her face.

"But, Tess," Miranda said, impulsively putting her arm around the older woman's shoulders, "whatever could you envy in me? You have everything a woman could want—a doting husband, three healthy children, a wonderful home."

"Exactly," Tess replied, averting her face from Miranda's view. She could not quite subdue the small grin of triumph that twitched at her charming lips. "But you cannot want such things. You have said often enough that a woman should not be limited to home and family. Are not you the one who quotes Mrs. Wollstonecraft to me? Women should be educated and treated as equals to men. Why else were they given brains? And you have shown that such views have merit. While I am but a silly female who must depend upon a man for fulfillment, you are able to stand on your own and do quite well. It is that that I envy in you."

"Oh, Tess," Miranda murmured, touched with chagrin at her cousin's revelations. "I never meant that it was wrong for women to want marriage, a home and a family, nor that such women were less than they ought to be. I only meant that it is wrong to deny women the right to rule their own lives. And since I am unlikely ever to find a man willing to grant me the independence I deem to be my right as a human being, I think it most unlikely that I shall ever marry.''

"But, Miranda," Tess cried, regarding her with a suddenly intent gaze, "does that mean that were you to find such a paragon and were he to offer for you, you would not spurn such a marriage?''

Miranda, feeling that she had somehow been outmaneuvered, withdrew her arm in sudden alarm. She rose nervously to her feet and retreated to the window to look out on the sweeping lawns surrounding the manor. Briefly she wished she might somehow escape the unpleasantness waiting for her below in the Queen's Saloon and ride Aster across the green countryside.

"Well, Miranda?" Tess pursued with the instincts of the born hunter.

Well aware that her cousin would not be put off without some sort of answer, the young woman sighed and turned away from the window.

"Of course, I should have to feel a certain affection for such a man," she said slowly. "And he for me."

"Naturally," Tess agreed. "So?"

"Oh, Tess!" Miranda cried in exasperation. "I am not without feelings. I want love just like anyone else. And children of my own. Of course I should consider such a marriage. But as it is unlikely I shall ever be in such a position, I find this conversation singularly unprofitable.''

"I, on the other hand, am glad you do not hold me or my kind in low esteem, Miranda," Tess countered soulfully. "And I cannot help but point out that you are in a remarkably advantageous position to advance the cause of women's rights in the succeeding days at Applegarth. For you will be in the company of three of the most noted misogynists in the realm. And all you need do is be yourself. They cannot help but see your undoubted femininity, and I shall take care that they become aware of your accomplishments. The combination will be proof enough that women are not the mindless ninnies men believe them to be."

"Tess, what are you saying?" Miranda asked, thoroughly alarmed now. "I will not be a part of any matchmaking scheme. Besides, you yourself have said I lack the countenance to interest the duke."

"Oh, I doubt that anyone could interest Evan for very long," Tess remarked guilelessly, but her eyes sparkled with interest at Miranda's singling out of the duke. "And I have said nothing of matchmaking. I merely pointed out that, have you the courage of your convictions, you can show these abominable bachelors the stuff of which women are made. Or do you not believe in what you've just said?"

"Of course I do. It's just that—"

"Very well, then. Let us begin. It is time for tea. And it is time you showed yourself. The others will be in the Queen's Saloon, I've no doubt."

Taking Miranda's arm, she led her unresisting from the room, little guessing with what real dread her cousin approached the inevitable meeting with the odious duke.

The Queen's Saloon, so named for having once briefly entertained the presence of Good Queen Bess on her way from London, seemed to Miranda to be crowded with elegantly clad people conversing pleasantly over dainty Sèvres teacups. As they entered, all conversation abruptly ceased, and Miranda found herself the cynosure of all eyes. Yet it was one pair of cynical blue orbs that brought the blood rushing to her cheeks and caused her to straighten her back. *He will not have the satisfaction of seeing me at my worst again,* she told herself and allowed a cool smile to play about her lips as she steeled herself to meet the assembled lords and ladies.

She was presented first to a lively young miss hardly out of the schoolroom, who regarded her with laughing brown eyes and a delightfully mischievous smile. Her name was Marian Horton and she was accompanied by a slender, well-knit youth in regimentals who was apparently possessed—judging from the firm jut of an angular jaw, the ponderous bulge in a noble brow beneath severely pomaded hair and the stern line of finely molded lips—of a singularly sober outlook on life. He stood rigidly at attention while Lady Davenforth introduced him to Miranda as Lieutenant Forsythe, on leave from the Royal Dragoons.

"Your servant, ma'am," he said, then nearly startled a giggle from Miranda as he clicked the heels of his gleaming Hessians smartly together and bowed stiffly over her hand.

"Oh, isn't Gregory marvelous, Miss Waincourt?" queried Miss Horton in a conspiratorial aside that nevertheless brought a faint tinge of color to the young officer's tanned cheeks. "We are to be married at the end of the month, and I am to follow the drum," she added with the air of one who has been promised a very special treat.

"Then I must wish you happy, Miss Horton," Miranda replied with a warm smile.

"Oh, I shall be. Thank you. You see, I have looked forward to it for ever so long. Gregory and I have known each other since I was a child. And I have never loved anyone else. It promises to be a perfectly marvelous adventure, so deliciously romantic following the drum to all sorts of exotic places, don't you agree?"

Miranda, who could not imagine anything less romantic than having to put up with the privations of the King's army in foreign parts, nodded gracious agreement. But Lieutenant Forsythe had other ideas.

"Marian, I have tried to make clear to you that it will not be at all romantic," he admonished sternly. "You are sure to be disappointed if you do not rid yourself of such nonsensical notions. The soldier's life is hard, and so is that of his loved ones who choose to follow him into danger."

"Have you been in foreign parts before, Lieutenant Forsythe?" politely inquired Miss Waincourt, who both approved of his attempt to inculcate more reasonable expectations in his bride-to-be and was amused by his attitude of mature superiority. She was surprised to see a slow blush suffuse his cheeks.

"Oh, no," piped up Miss Horton. "Sir Godfrey, Gregory's father, has only just purchased his colors. But Gregory has studied shelffuls of books about the army. He knows simply everything there is to know."

"No doubt," commented Miss Waincourt, feeling suddenly quite ancient, and allowed herself to be led away to meet a pleasant middle-aged couple who greeted her with a friendly warmth that set her immediately at her ease. They were Lord and Lady Crenshawe, and they were pleased to inform her that they had known her mother when she made her come-out so many years before. Miranda would have been content to stay the rest of the afternoon listening to Lady Crenshawe talk about her mama as a young girl, but Lady Tess firmly disengaged her cousin and steered her toward the remaining lady in the room.

Lady Horton, an imposing dowager with steel-gray hair beneath an impressive lavender turban topped by three awesome ostrich feathers, extended two fingers.

"I am glad to see you recovered from your indisposition, my dear," she said in greeting. "You are most fortunate, from what I have heard, not to have suffered anything more serious than a cold. Most courageous of you, I'm sure, to have attempted the rescue of Eversley's cattle, but hardly wise, don't you think? Such things were better left to men. Don't you agree, Lady Davenforth?"

"Oh, but Miranda has a wonderful hand with horses, Lady Horton. Why, her stables are renowned all over England. I do not think a man could have done better in such an emergency. And I feel sure Eversley was glad of her assistance under the circumstances."

"Indeed?" queried the dowager and lifted her lorgnette to observe Miranda better. As if she were some odd creature dragged in from the wilds of India, thought Miranda dourly, and suppressed the grimace of distaste with which she longed to meet the dowager's pointed scrutiny.

"Oh, indeed, Lady Horton," chimed in a new voice, one remarkable for its deep, drawling baritone. Miranda glanced incredulously into the indolent face of the duke. Immediately she dropped her eyes to hide the spark of resentment that had been ignited by his mocking smile. "Miss Waincourt was of invaluable aid. Despite my fear that her impetuous actions would lead to her injury, she proved amazingly adept. Quite unlike the usual miss, she was not only able to gentle the frightened animal, but was equally capable of caring for my injured tiger. And for that I am most humbly grateful."

"Oh! How is the boy?" Miranda exclaimed, ashamed that in all the confusion of the past two days she had quite forgotten about the tiger.

"As well as you, it would seem," responded the duke with a smile. "He is up and around. Thankfully, he was not seriously concussed."

"I'm glad. He lay still for so long, I was afraid he might never recover."

"I must protest, Eversley. You are shamefully monopolizing this quite intriguing young woman," remarked a smooth voice at Miranda's elbow.

She turned to meet the amused glance of a gentleman of medium height. He was nattily dressed in a brown single-breasted coat that hugged muscular shoulders. A striped waistcoat with a single gold fob was accentuated by an immaculate white neckcloth tied in the Mathematical. Buff gaiter pantaloons seemed molded to powerful thighs. He was not handsome, his features lacking the regularity that marked the striking good looks of the duke. Gray eyes seemed to look upon the world with constant amusement. A long nose with flaring nostrils, a full mustache that met long sandy sideburns, and a wide mouth on which a humorous smile forever hovered, created an arresting countenance that was not unpleasant to look upon.

Instinctively Miranda knew that here was the second of the "Inconquerables."

"Quite so, Chester," the duke was saying in a bland voice. "A circumstance that I alter only because civility demands it. Allow me to introduce you to Miss Miranda Waincourt, sister to the Earl of Waring. Miss Waincourt: Chester Harkness, Earl of Chomney."

"Miss Waincourt, a pleasure indeed. How is it that we've not met before? I cannot believe I should ever forget such a delectable creature," he said, observing her with a flattering glance from head to toe.

Miranda, who was able from her willowy height to look straight into his laughing eyes, returned his gaze in like manner. "I cannot say, my lord, except that I've led a cloistered life at Groves and can only affirm that we have never before encountered one another. I can assure you that neither could I have forgotten such a singular meeting as that must have been."

The earl bowed from the waist in acknowledgement of a palpable hit and smiled broadly, revealing large, even white teeth with a gap between the front two. "Definitely not in the usual style. Eh, Eversley? I can see Charles's house party promises to be more amusing than I had anticipated."

"Then allow me to join in the fun," entreated a third gentleman, who managed by sheer height to edge Eversley aside. Miranda looked up into a long face remarkable for its ruddy complexion and thoughtful pale blue eyes. He had straight blond hair parted in the middle and swept back from a high forehead. Thin lips parted over crooked, rather yellow teeth in a nevertheless engaging grin. He was quite the tallest man Miranda had ever seen, topping the duke's considerable height by two inches at least. And while his shoulders were broad, he had a gangling appearance due, no doubt, to his rather loose-fitting day coat of a light shade of green known as "parsley mixture." Cream-colored breeches hugged slender thighs, which, despite their lack of girth, appeared muscular. Knee-high Hessians displaying an indifferent gloss declared an apparent lack of interest in his appearance. Here was a man who clearly valued comfort over fashion, Miranda judged and liked him immediately.

"But, Jeremy, what possible interest could a noted misogynist such as yourself have in the lovely Miss Waincourt?" queried Chomney, a mischievous glint in his gray eyes.

"Damme, Chums," said the gentleman in the most drawn-out drawl Miranda had ever heard, "whoever said I hated women? Not so. Women beautify a place, which is doubly needed when you're about. Allow me to introduce m'self, Miss Waincourt. Jeremy Bannington, Marquess of Pulvney. Your servant, ma'am."

"My lord," Miranda responded sweetly and dropped a curtsy to the third of the "Inconquerables."

CHAPTER SEVEN

MIRANDA COULD NEVER afterward determine why she
suddenly found herself the center of attention of the
three most renowned bachelors in the realm, and yet
she was never to emerge from her chamber but that
one or more of the three swarmed to her side like
honeybees to a delectable blossom. Indeed, were she
not quite sure they were merely attempting to relieve
the boredom of three town beaux cut off from the
more alluring entertainments of London, she doubted
not that her head would have grown quite oversized
with vanity.

As it was, she found herself enjoying her illusory
popularity, which she viewed as a delightful game far
removed from the reality to which she must soon return upon leaving Applegarth for Groves. She maintained a cool but amiable distance that, had she but
known it, was far more intriguing to men used to the
coquettish ploys of the maiden in hot pursuit of a
match. She was used to say whatever came to her mind
with a candor that would have put to the blush her
more decorous contemporaries. Nor did she succumb
to the practiced blandishments of the three gentlemen, who were all noted for their deadly charm and

undeniable eligibility. She was judged unaffected, witty and something of an original.

In short, Miranda was having the time of her life.

She quite forgot in the heady pleasure of measuring her wits against three accomplished flirts the nefarious scheme of her cousin Tess. She might have been excused for so fatal an oversight by the mere fact of her inexperience. After all, what did she know of matters of the heart?

Thus she failed to note with due seriousness the growing attentiveness of the Marquess of Pulvney, whose developing habit of looking fixedly at her for long, pregnant moments—rather like a hapless bird entranced by the hypnotic stare of the cobra, Eversley was heard to say with a sardonic curl of his handsome lips—she was wont to attribute to his rather ponderous nature. For, while Chomney was noted for his levity and flirtatious wit, Pulvney was like to respond to conversational exchanges with a thoughtful silence that would eventually give birth to a quite apt response in his exceedingly protracted drawl. He never answered without first giving the matter its due consideration. He was, consequently, a favorite target for his more quick-witted friend, the Earl of Chomney, who, on the surface at least, was pursuing the elusive Miss Waincourt with the determination of a hound on the scent.

Eversley, too, paid the self-avowed spinster the dubious honor of his polished attentions. Much to Miranda's chagrin and evident disgust, the duke, whenever either or both of his friends had contrived to take her apart from the rest of the company at Applegarth, was wont to intrude his presence upon them. Nor was she ever allowed private discourse with either of her swains. He was, she suspicioned, bent on protecting his fellow Inconquerables from an unscrupulous female determined to ensnare one or both in her supposed matrimonial coils. He was unfailingly proper in his conduct toward her, displaying a deadly charm, which, had she not known his true character, might have proved as devastating to her as it had to many another less knowledgeable female. She, in turn, treated him to a cool disdain in sharp contrast to the friendly regard with which she met the advances of her other two beaux.

One day Miranda emerged from her chamber becomingly gowned in a mint-green morning dress of sprigged muslin that Madame Tusseaud had completed only the day before, and wended her way to the breakfast room, which she hoped she might have to herself, as she had risen unfashionably early for that very purpose. While she enjoyed the flattering attention she had been receiving, the need to be ever witty and alert was taking its toll on her customary unfemininely hearty appetite. In short, she found it difficult to eat when she must be forever responding adroitly to the gay repartee of her dinner companions. She doubted not that were her stay to be an extended one, she should be doomed to waste away to nothing. Moreover, she was beginning to miss the easy informality and undeniable uproar of meals taken in the family dining room at Groves. Thus she regarded the presence of the Duke of Eversley lingering over his morning coffee and the most recent London paper to reach the barren fastness of the country with a pang of displeasure that she had difficulty in concealing.

"Whatever are you doing here?" she exclaimed before she thought, then, blushing furiously, sought to retrieve her strategical error. "I—I mean, I had not thought to encounter anyone about. It is somewhat in advance of your customary hour of rising, is it not?"

"Oh, unquestionably," he replied with a hint of amusement in the sleepy blue eyes as he leisurely rose to make her an ironic bow. "You, on the other hand, no doubt make it a habit to greet the birds, Miss Waincourt. One's duty is a deuced hard taskmaster, after all."

"Something which you would know nothing about," she retorted, then clapped one hand to her mouth. "Oh, you really are quite abominable," she said ruefully. "You are determined to bring out the worst in me. But I refuse to be baited before I have broken my fast and so do most humbly beg your pardon for my uncivil remark."

"Peace it is, then, Miss Waincourt," he agreed affably, though an odd expression flitted briefly across his countenance. Miranda tried not to fidget under his hooded gaze and at last allowed a short, rather nervous laugh to bubble forth.

"I beg you will be seated," she said in no little exasperation at his protracted scrutiny of her. "I have no wish to disturb your reading. Pay me no mind. I shall simply serve myself."

"As you wish, ma'am," he replied and obligingly returned to his newspaper.

Miranda helped herself to a goodly portion of grilled kidneys, scrambled eggs and toast and took a seat across from the odious duke. Determined not to allow his disturbing presence to interfere with the appeasement of her appetite, she poured black coffee and proceeded to do justice to the hearty breakfast with which she had supplied herself.

When at last she had taken the sharp edge off her hunger and leaned back with a low sigh to sip at her coffee, she noticed the duke regarding her with amusement.

"Are you always such an enthusiastic trencherwoman, Miss Waincourt? Or has the delightful Lady Tess only just released you from her prescribed diet of broth and weak tea? Oh, no. Do not fly up into the boughs. I find an honest appetite in one of your sex refreshing. Do you care to look over the paper?"

Miranda stifled the gasp that rose to her lips at his rude observation and waved aside the society page that he had offered her.

"If you have finished reading the news of the City," she said ingenuously, "I should like to catch up on the stock market."

The arrogant brows rose a fraction of an inch.

"Are you a speculator, Miss Waincourt?" he queried with a sardonic curl of the finely molded lips.

"No, Your Grace," the lady responded with a flash of cool green eyes, "I am a British subject, and as such have an understandable interest in all that concerns my country."

"Indeed, then perhaps you have an opinion on the French tyrant's latest decree of November. Do you think he will be successful in his economic campaign against England?''

''I think his Continental System will never stop British trade, my lord Duke. There will always be those willing to carry British goods in spite of all the tyrant's decrees. Besides which, the European continent as exemplified by the Portuguese, the Spanish and the Dutch, who depend on English trade, and the Russians, who look to us for a market for their timber and flax, will never stand for it. He will be forced to invade Russia, and the Great Bear of the North will not prove an easy victim even to his hitherto victorious armies.''

''You may be right. The English smuggler is a clever fellow and will not be easily discouraged from plying his trade. But have you, I wonder, taken into account the unfortunate circumstance that an England without timber is an England without ships?'' observed Eversley thoughtfully, his gaze never once leaving the animated face of his companion. ''Without Prussian oak we may indeed find ourselves in a serious coil.''

''Perhaps,'' the lady replied, her smooth brow furrowing as she wrestled with this new problem in world politics. ''And yet Bonaparte suffers from a serious flaw. I do not think he will wait for British shipping to founder from want of timber, for Wellington himself has said the Emperor has not the patience for a defensive war.''

''How very intriguing,'' murmured the duke enigmatically. ''How do you come to be so well informed, Miss Waincourt? You do not strike me as the type to wear blue stockings.''

Miranda's resentful glance flew to the duke's face.

"Oh, I am shockingly unfashionable, my lord Duke," she said with a toss of her coppery curls. "I do not hesitate to declare myself quite bookish. A meaningful education being denied most members of my sex, I was fortunate my father allowed me free access to his library, for which he had very little use himself. No doubt if he had had any notion of the extent of my studies, he would have forbidden me further use of his books on the grounds that a delicately bred female should be allowed only such knowledge as makes her company pleasing to men and herself suitable to run a household. But you must forgive him this oversight in his fatherly duties. He was much too busy attempting to send us all down the River Tick with his mounting debts of honor to pay attention to the immodest pursuits of his elder daughter. Now, if you will excuse me, I shall leave you to your coffee."

She rose abruptly from the table and turned preparatory to sweeping from the room in a high dudgeon, only to have her wrist imprisoned by the duke's slender hand.

"I beg your pardon, Miss Waincourt," he said quietly. "I meant no aspersion to your character. Indeed, I enjoyed our discussion exceedingly. It is unusual to encounter a female content to let one enjoy one's morning paper in silence and then proving an interesting conversationalist into the bargain. I should hope we might continue the discussion at another time."

Miranda, feeling as though somehow the world had gone topsy-turvy, stared in startled disbelief at the handsome face above her own and could read nothing there but sincere warmth.

"No-o," she answered uncertainly, confusion at his sudden change in attitude making it difficult to think clearly. "It is I who should apologize. I have the lamentable habit of overreacting to criticism of my sex."

"No, no, my dear. You must not retreat from a stand that has right on its side. It would not be in character, and I have come to expect honesty from you. I should not like to be disappointed."

"Should you not?" she queried in a suddenly weak voice, all too aware of his proximity. She thought she might succumb to a fit of the vapors if she did not soon escape his disturbing presence, and she could not prevent a softly pleading look from darkening her eyes.

He held her for an endless moment with his intense blue gaze, then, uttering a short, oddly husky bark of laughter, he released her and stepped back, the indolent mask of the town beau descending over his features.

She was saved from having to discover a graceful means of withdrawing by the sudden entrance of the Earl of Chomney, whose gaze narrowed suspiciously at the interesting aspect of the duke and the intriguing Miss Waincourt alone together in the breakfast room. Miranda, grateful to be rescued, awarded the earl a melting look, which brought his lordship immediately to her side. Taking up her hand in his, he brushed the knuckles with his lips and smiled into her eyes.

"My delectable Miss Waincourt. What an enchanting way to begin the day. Just say the word, and we shall make it a permanent arrangement. What say you, m'dear?"

"I say you are a charming rogue who would run at the first sign of my accepting your proposal." Miranda laughed and withdrew her hand.

"Do not be too sure of that," he answered, and Miranda blushed at the suddenly intent look in his eyes. Thus neither saw the duke suddenly stiffen and bend a penetrating glance upon the two.

"Ah, Chomney," he remarked in a velvety voice, "as dependable as always. And where, I cannot help but wonder, is the inescapable Pulvney? One cannot hope to see the one without the other when Miss Waincourt is about."

"I cannot speak for Jeremy, but I have risen at this wholly preposterous hour in the hopes of engaging Miss Waincourt for an afternoon's outing. What say you, m'dear, to a drive down to the village?" Then, at Miranda's apparent hesitation, he grinned engagingly and added in a conspiratorial undertone, "I warn you, I am not averse to stooping to bribery. I promise to let you tool my matched set of bays, the sweetest goers in the realm, notwithstanding Eversley's overrated chestnuts."

"But how rash of you," remarked the duke blandly. "I fear I have no recourse but to demand satisfaction for so patent an untruth. My chestnuts against your bays, Chomney. Winner take all."

"Here, here, now. What's all this?" queried the bluff voice of Sir Charles Davenforth, who had entered unnoticed by his three guests. He was attired in a bottle-green riding coat and buff unmentionables and apparently had just returned from an early-morning ride. "This sounds deadly serious."

"Absurd, is more like," Miranda observed with a darkling glance at the duke. "But then it is a matter of an honorable wager between gentlemen, is it not?"

"Quite so, my dear," Eversley replied with a slight curl of the lips.

"Oh! And I, a woman, have no say in the matter, I suppose."

"But of course you have not, Miranda," Sir Charles foolishly interjected. "This is hardly a matter to concern a female."

"But it does concern me. The wager stems, after all, from Lord Chomney's kind offer to let me drive his bays. It is just the sort of nonsense I have learned to abhor in gentlemen."

"Now, Miranda," Sir Charles said uneasily. "You are understandably upset. We all know how you feel about your father's—er—I mean t'say, this is no place for a female of delicate sensibilities. You would be better served to join Tess in the nursery. She was asking for you, y'know."

"Oh, the devil fly away with your notions of the proper place for females," Miranda uttered in exasperation at the insufferable attitude of male superiority surrounding her on three sides. "I have no doubt that neither of these gentlemen could touch my team of grays in a fair race. But I am not so foolish as to risk the livelihood of my family on a foolish bet. That, in *my* view, would be lacking in all honor."

"Ah, but what of the honor of the Waincourt name, m'dear?" Chomney queried, his eyes alight with mischief. "Would it not bring you satisfaction to prove your faith in the Waincourt breed of cattle? And if, after all, you are sure of your ability to win, what real risk do you take?"

"The risk that every gamester runs who believes he shall make all come about on the next turn of the card," Miranda answered bitterly. "I believe that there are no finer cattle in all of England than mine. But one cannot take into account the vagaries of fate: a broken axle, an unexpected obstacle in the road. One can never be sure of winning."

"Oh, but I can," said the duke. "And to prove it, I withdraw my stakes and wager instead my chestnuts against a single lock of your hair that my team will take yours. What say you, Miss Waincourt? Have you the courage of your convictions?"

"Now, hold on, Evan. The wager was with me."

"I see no reason to alter our arrangement, Chomney. But this is a matter between Miss Waincourt and myself."

"Not very chivalrous, old boy," Sir Charles remarked with the air of one faced with disaster. Tess would raise the very devil over this morning's work. "Miss Waincourt can hardly take such a proposition seriously. It would sink her beneath reproach."

"Oh, but I do take it seriously," Miss Waincourt answered with a flash of emerald eyes. "If Charles will be so kind as to lend me the use of his racing curricle, I accept your terms!"

"BUT, MIRANDA, you cannot be serious!" a much distraught Lady Tess cried later that morning as she faced her determined cousin after having run her down at last in the rose garden. "Lady Horton will not hesitate to spread the tale to every withdrawing room in the realm. Your reputation will be utterly ruined. You won't be able to show your face in polite society again."

"Oh, it was foolish, I've no doubt. But what's done is done. I will not back out now. At any rate, I arrived with my reputation in shatters. I can hardly be worse off. And it was our intent to prove that women are equal in every way to men, was it not?"

"It was, of course," her cousin reluctantly agreed, "but I never dreamed it would go so far. Miranda, you cannot realize what you are risking."

"I am risking a lock of my hair. I fail to see the enormity of that."

"You are risking far more than that, if you can only be brought to see it. How can you be so blind? Pulvney is within an inch of coming up to scratch. And Chomney, too, has shown a marked interest. I shouldn't wonder if he didn't make an offer as well. And Evan: I've never known him to look at a woman as he looks at you."

"Like a cat at a canary, you mean. Well, I do not care for the duke's look, and I do not propose to be so easily swallowed up," she retorted and then turned sharply away from Tess's discerning eye to hide the sudden surge of emotion that flitted across her face. For just a moment that morning, before Chomney's disastrous entrance, she had liked the duke's look very well indeed. In fact, she was very sure she had quite misjudged the arrogant nobleman. But then he had changed and goaded her, deliberately, she doubted not, into her unwise acceptance of his wager. She did not need Tess to tell her how badly she had erred. And though she already regretted her hasty decision, she little relished the idea of crying off, for it would mean humbling herself before the arrogant duke. Oh, how he would enjoy that! she thought miserably.

"Well, if you will not consider yourself, Miranda," Tess pleaded, "at least think what it will do to me. A scandal such as this will ruin me as a hostess. I will never be able to show my face in town again, let alone expect the ton to flock to my parties as they were used to do. Miranda, I beg you to reconsider."

"Oh, my poor Tess!" Miranda cried in chagrin. "I never thought of that. And yet I cannot believe anyone could hold you responsible for what has happened. You must simply disavow any connection with me. Put it all on my head. Claim you did all in your power to stop me but that I simply would not listen to reason."

"A fine friend that would make me," said Tess with a firm toss of her blond curls. "No. I shall stand by you, Miranda, come what may. I ask only that you reconsider. It is truly you I am concerned about."

With that, Lady Tess gave her cousin a quick hug and left Miranda to wrestle with her uneasy conscience. Only then did she really consider what Tess had said about Pulvney and Chomney. The idea that either one or both might be near a declaration was indeed a sobering thought. She could place little credence in Chomney's alleged serious intent. He was, she judged, a charming rogue and nothing more. But Pulvney was a different proposition altogether.

For a moment she tried to imagine herself married to the gentle marquess. He would be kind to her and would not be an onerous taskmaster. He recognized her serious side and her need for independence and would not object to allowing her a certain degree of freedom. He enjoyed her wit and encouraged her to share her opinions with him, listening with a touching gravity that had nothing of condescension about it. He seemed in every way but one the perfect candidate for her hand. He had little patience with children, shunning the idea of Tess's three enchanting hooligans with a charming shiver of distaste. He would little take to the idea of welcoming her three younger siblings into his home, let alone poor Aunt Agatha. And she simply could not abandon them to the careless guardianship of her rascally eldest brother. Indeed, had Henry Waincourt been a paragon among brothers, she could never have given up her dear Allie, whom she had regarded as her own since first she held the motherless babe in her arms. She simply could not in all conscience condemn dear Jeremy to marriage with her. He deserved better.

No, she would not marry Pulvney, she thought, and Chomney could not be truly seriously considering offering for her. And as for the duke, well, her cousin was well off the mark if she honestly thought Miranda had aroused any interest in that quarter other than a total disgust for the impudent spinster whom he himself had categorized as a provincial without countenance or polish. And yet...

Suddenly she was haunted by cerulean eyes beneath indolent lids and could not banish from her mind the strange warmth he had had for her in his gaze just before Chomney had intruded on them. She remembered with pleasure their earlier conversation and how easy it had been to forget herself with this man. Nor had he been put off by her temerity in speaking of things usually considered beyond the proper understanding of a woman. What an odd man he was, to be sure: one minute to tease her unmercifully and the next to applaud her honesty. Oh, why could she not learn to govern her wayward tongue? She had interfered where she had had no right to, and now she was to play the fool again and to drag her well-meaning cousin down with her. She had certainly made a proper mull of everything, she thought miserably.

Well, it was not too late to put an end to it. She had heard him tell Sir Charles he must see him in the library at eleven. If she hurried, she might yet catch him there. She fled into the house, acknowledging Lady Horton's imperious greeting from the Queen's Saloon with a polite nod and hurrying on down the hall to pause at last in order to catch her breath before making her presence known to those within the library.

The door was slightly ajar, and Sir Charles's voice carried easily to her.

"Damme, Evan. You've created a pretty coil. 'Tis bad enough that you lure me into agreeing to wager my mare against your gray hunter that you'd have

Miranda eating out of your hand in a fortnight. And so far as I am concerned the wager is off, though it looks as if pigs'll fly before ever you get that female to call you 'Evan, darling.' But now you must put up your matched chestnuts against a lock of her hair. You'll ruin the gel, and all because you suspect that my wife brought you here to lure you into matrimony. Surely you do not mean to go through with this far-adiddle of nonsense?''

"But of course I shall go through with it," replied the duke, his deep voice vibrant with amusement. "And I fully intend to win a lock of hair from the confirmed spinster. After all, so avowed a man-hater must not be disappointed. But Miss Waincourt's name will not suffer for it, I assure you."

"And how do you propose to avoid the inevitable? I find it difficult to believe even you could persuade Lady Horton to hold her tongue."

"I very much doubt, my friend, that even the re-doubtable Lady Horton will care to impugn the rep-utation of the Duchess of Eversley. Or do you feel my credit is not great enough to carry us all through this afternoon's proposed farce?''

"The Duchess of Eversley?" echoed a suddenly bemused Sir Charles. "Egad! D'you mean to wed the gel?''

"It has been my intention since a certain im-promptu picnic in your very own library, dear Charles. I had come to believe there could never be a woman like the incomparable Miss Waincourt. No doubt your clever lady wife will be in alt to learn that at last she has found the means of conquering the Inconquerable,'' he ended with a hearty chuckle, but unfortunately the incomparable Miss Waincourt never heard it, for she had fled in a cold fury up the stairs upon hearing his apparently brazen admission of culpability in scheming to bring about her downfall.

CHAPTER EIGHT

THE AFTERNOON, observed Lady Tess with abhorrence, was disgustingly lovely, with neither a whisper of a breeze nor a suggestion of the devoutly hoped-for rain cloud to mar its perfection. Well, perhaps permanent retirement to the country would not be totally without reward. Surely, in her purely selfless attempt to obtain the happiness of two of her best-loved people, she would earn a heavenly recompence for the sacrifice of her name and reputation as a hostess, though she rather suspected that the dubious distinction of sainthood would not help to alleviate the tedium of an eternity spent in the country. Yet she had only herself to blame, for had not Charles warned her often enough that one day she would be made to pay for her matchmaking schemes? Oh, if only she had listened to him! Henceforth she would regard his every word as an inarguable piece of wisdom. She would become the exemplary wife, and perhaps one day she would be forgiven her transgressions. She was quite sure she should never be able to hold up her head again after Lady Horton had done her work in spreading the news of Lady Davenforth's scandalous house party, but perhaps, when she was a very old and decrepit woman, she might be allowed to attend again a very occasional musicale or even to sit with the other dowagers on the sidelines at a rout in town. It was, after all, the most she could hope for under the circumstances.

Miranda, seething at the perfidy of all men in general and the duke in particular, was unaware of her cousin's sudden repentance or her aspirations for ultimate redemption. She was perched on the driver's seat of Sir Charles's recently purchased riding curricle, two exceedingly fresh prime bloods chomping at the bits in their traces. Having yet to receive from Madame Tusseaud the new habit, which was promised on the morrow, she was attired in an outmoded one of indiscriminate drab green that had seen much service over the years. Over her fiery curls she had thrust a broad-brimmed beaver which had once belonged to her elder brother, and which she had attempted to beautify with a curling ostrich feather. All in all, she must present a disreputable sight, she thought wryly, and did not care a whit, for after this day she would be as disreputable as her appearance. But she would be returning home with a nice addition to her stables and the satisfaction of having bested the odious duke at his own game, she consoled herself.

Sir Charles had chosen a ten-mile course of country roads and tracks that began at the iron gates to Applegarth and proceeded south to follow the Medway River east for a time before swinging north again and home.

"Watch out for the wooded stretch just south of the gates," he said with a meaningful glance at Miranda. "The road winds through the trees and is too narrow to allow you to pass one another till you reach the open land beyond. May the best man—er—driver win.''

Then, with an eye to his watch, he raised the starting gun and counted off the seconds to the starting time.

As the gun went off, Miranda's off-side horse reared, dragging his mate with him. Instantly she steadied them with firm, sensitive hands on the lines, so that they came down running. Chomney's bays took the lead, with Eversley holding a steady pace to his rear. Miranda let out the reins and gave the grays their heads for a pace until they reached the woods a half-mile down the road. The duke was a carriage length ahead as she pulled back, content to let the others set the pace around the hazardous turns. The grays were running well, and Miranda experienced an exhilarating calm as she was caught up in the race. Forgotten were all thoughts of her ruined reputation or her revenge against the duke. She was conscious only of the trees whipping past her in a blur, the wind against her face and the need to hold steady to the curves.

Then suddenly the woods were behind her, giving way to rolling pastureland. She glimpsed Chomney making his move to lengthen his lead, but the duke held back. She could see him talking to his pair, holding them as they fought to take the bit. She closed the distance between them, then settled in behind, letting Eversley's curricle block for her and pull her team along in the drag.

Chomney was a quarter-mile ahead when the road began to climb a long hill hedged on either side by a low stone wall. Miranda could see the bays strain against the traces and silently applauded the duke's strategy. Chomney's team would reach the top already winded while the other two teams had yet to work up a lather. She saw the earl's arm rise and fall as he began to apply the whip. Then he was over the top and sinking out of sight on the downgrade.

The grays took to the incline, pulling easily. She called to them and let them have their heads. Then she heard the duke's deep voice shout her name. She glanced up to see a farm cart pulled by an ancient plow horse topping the rise and coming toward them. She pulled her team sharply to the left and hugged the wall. The duke whisked neatly past the cart with bare inches to spare, but the startled nag drawing the cart shied and swerved toward Miranda, the frightened farmer shaking his fist at her. She sawed farther to the left, letting the wheel scrape the wall. Then she was past and running smoothly again, the top of the rise just before her.

Once on the downgrade, she risked a glance ahead. The earl had lengthened the lead to half a mile, but he was using the whip steadily, and beyond him the road curved to follow the river. Now! she thought and called to the leaders, just as Eversley lowered the reins and let the chestnuts out. One behind the other, they swept down the hill, matching each other pace for pace. Chomney had entered the long curve when the duke feathered the corner and swept past, Miranda on his heels.

"Take him, lass!" Chomney cried, and she grinned at the sound of his wild shout of laughter. Then she forgot him as she entered a series of sharp turns.

Eversley did not let up on the pace as she had expected him to do, and Miranda thrilled as she saw him neatly feather curve after curve. She knew then why they called him the nonpareil. Yet she was no mere whipster. Abandoning caution, she clung to his heels, working her team around each bend with a daring that was well known to her intimates and that had been the despair of John Coachman since first he had put her behind a team at the age of twelve. If the duke had thought to lose her in the treacherous turns, he was to be disappointed, for abruptly the track straightened and headed north again around the base of the hill that had cost Chomney the race.

They were past the halfway mark and heading home with perhaps two miles of wide-open country before them until they entered the woods again. It was now or never, Miranda thought and let out a wild pealing cry. The grays lunged forward, stretching out into the mile-eating pace for which they had been bred. The distance between Miranda's pair and Eversley's curricle closed. The grays nosed past the wheels, then drew abreast of the duke's chestnuts. Out of the corner of her eye she saw Eversley drop his hands, she heard him call to his team, and still Miranda steadily gained. Then the two pairs were running neck and neck and it seemed that neither would pull ahead.

Now he'll take to the whip, she thought and was startled to see him pulling back on the reins. The grays shot ahead, and Miranda looked up to see the woods scant yards before them. With a low cry she yawed to the left directly in front of the duke and thundered into the narrow track weaving among the trees. She had him! She had won. And yet she felt somehow cheated. Realizing she had not seen her peril, he had pulled back to let her on the track again. He dared not pass her now. Yet suddenly there he was, cutting off her lead from the right. He must have left the narrow track as it curved, she thought with reluctant admiration. Taking a straight course through the trees, he whipped past her and came back to the road in the lead. Then they were out of the woods with the gates of Applegarth before them. Eversley had won.

Miranda swept through the gates and pulled her lathered team to a walk. She saw the duke salute her and returned the gallant gesture with a cool nod. Then John Coachman was there to take the near horse's head, and Pulvney was helping her down from the curricle.

"Walk them till they're cool," she said unnecessarily. The groom had taught her all she knew about horses, but she needed to talk, and, hardly aware of the marquess striding beside her, she turned to walk with her old friend and retainer toward the stables.

"He never beat them," she stated, as though it were the groom who needed reassurance. "They're hardly winded. It was I who lost the race. He's the best I've ever seen. No one else would have dared cut through the trees the way he did. No one else could have pulled it off."

"Aye, Miss Miranda. He be right handy. But ye give 'im a race. And loike as not 'e'd not work th' same trick on ye twicet. Ye've naught t' be ashamed on, I reckon.''

"If only the rest of the world would see it as you do, my friend." She laughed ruefully. "I've properly disgraced myself, I fear."

"Nonsense, Miss Waincourt," interjected the marquess in his slow drawl. With a start she realized she had forgotten him. "You were marvelous. Sorry I didn't think to warn you about Evan. Full of tricks, Evan is. Never known anyone to get the best of him in a race. Can't imagine why Chums egged him on. Must have known he'd never a chance of winning. Ain't so lack-witted as a rule."

"Isn't he, though?" Miranda queried, suddenly suspicious.

"Not so you'd notice," reflected the marquess. "I fancied he'd given up years ago ever hoping to beat Evan at anything, except now and then a woman they'd both an eye for. But you never can tell with those two. As for myself, I was never much in the petticoat line till quite recently." Miranda lowered her eyes in sudden uneasiness as the tall nobleman glanced significantly down at her. Then she realized he had pulled her aside and the groom had led the horses on, leaving her alone with Pulvney.

"Not till I met you, Miss Waincourt," the marquess said softly.

"My lord," Miranda began uncertainly, but Pulvney stopped her with a fingertip placed lightly against her lips.

"No, wait," he said quietly. "I know this is neither the time nor the place, but suddenly I feel I must speak. You must know, my dear, that I've come to love you and I want you for my wife. You needn't answer me now. Indeed, I'd rather you didn't. Think on it, and if you feel you could be happy with a slow top like myself, you'd make me the happiest man in the realm. And now I see Lady Tess looking for you. I'll leave you in her care for the time being.''

Gently he placed a hand beneath her chin and forced her to look at him. His peculiarly sweet smile curved his lips as slowly he shook his head at her.

"Now don't you fret your pretty little head. Evan, Chums and I'll see to it that you're not hurt by this day's foolery. You'll be the toast of the town by the time we're through with the telling of this tale, I promise you.''

Then he was gone, and Miranda was left to soothe her cousin's jangled nerves.

"BUT YOU WILL NOT give him a lock of your hair, Miranda!'' Tess exclaimed as she faced her cousin in Miranda's bedchamber. It had come to her as she waited to see the outcome of the race that perhaps all was not so bleak as she had at first supposed. Actually, it had been Jeremy who had suggested they distract Lady Horton from her determination to condemn Miranda for an unruly hoyden by throwing a ball for, it seemed, almost the entire county. Surely, in the resulting confusion inherent in all such grand undertakings, the old gadfly would find something new to divert her flapping tongue. If only Miranda could be kept from further disgrace until the night of the ball. Yet here she had found her young cousin determined upon a course of ruination.

"It is a debt of honor, Tess," Miranda said wryly. "I have no choice but to pay up. At least it is only my hair he shall have," she added darkly, thinking of the wager that had brought him to Applegarth in the first place. How easily he had fooled her with his warm looks and false words of approval. No wonder he had changed so radically at the inn once he had learned who she was. The snake, to seek to charm her! And that touching scene in the library. Even then he had only been trying to trick her into an intimacy that would have won him his wager. How he must have chafed to think she had almost turned the tables on him, believing as he had that she had staged the whole incident in order to compromise him into offering for her. Oh, but he was abominable! Well, she would pay her debt to him, and then she would pack her trunk and return to Groves where she belonged, she decided with an oddly heavy heart, then became aware that Tess had been speaking to her for some time. She blinked and stared blankly at her cousin.

"I beg your pardon. I'm afraid I was woolgathering. What did you say?"

"I was saying that Jeremy has come up with a brilliant plan to head off Lady Horton and her wagging tongue. We shall have a ball. Almost the whole county will be invited. But it must be something very out of the ordinary, you understand. Now let me see. What can we do that has not been done before?" Tess mused, with one finger placed to her pursed lips.

"Well, I know very little about such things," Miranda observed a little impatiently. She had much rather be left to herself to contemplate the upsetting events of the day than plan a ball she would never attend. Not only had she Eversley to face one last time, but she must also find the words to refuse Pulvney's very touching offer without hurting him. And she had left Groves to escape her problems for a time! she thought ironically. How uncomplicated her life at home now seemed.

"Miranda, you are not attending me," Tess complained, regarding her cousin with a prettily arched eyebrow. "What do you say to a masked ball? Of course, that in itself would not be extraordinary, but if we were to assign it a theme, perhaps? Well, what do you think?"

"What do I think about what?"

"A theme, of course. Really, we are going to get nowhere if you do not begin to grasp the seriousness of this undertaking. We simply must distract Lady Horton if we are not both to be utterly ruined."

Miranda experienced a sudden stab of guilt as she met her cousin's troubled glance. It was her fault Tess faced the ostracism of the ton, and to Tess that would mean a punishment worse than death. With a sinking heart she realized she could not selfishly abandon her cousin to her fate. Stoically she turned her mind from her own troubles in order to come up with a theme for the proposed ball.

Suddenly her eyes fell on a small bust of Apollo that adorned her dressing table, and she uttered the first thought that came to her mind.

"Why not a classical theme?" she said. "We could all dress as Greek gods or goddesses."

"But that's been done before," Tess demurred, waving her hands in despair. "Everything's been done before. No doubt it is foolish to even imagine that we could divert the old gadfly. We shall simply have to brave it through as best we can and hope everything will be forgotten in a decade or two."

Miranda could not quite suppress a grin at Lady Tess's tragic pose, and yet she felt compelled to alleviate her cousin's very real distress.

"Oh, we shall not just dress as deities. We shall go a step further and require that each guest depict a myth. We can set up a panel of judges to decide who best portray their chosen tales and award the winners some sort of prize. Don't you see? Everyone will be quite diverted trying to guess what and whom each of us is trying to represent. It will be a sort of game."

"But that's a marvelous idea!" Tess cried, her blue eyes sparkling with sudden excitement. "We shall have Reverend Morseby to judge. And Lady Horton! That should give her something to think about other than that unfortunate race. Oh, you are a genius, Miranda! And it is just as well that we picked that Grecian robe for your ball gown. It should do perfectly for you, my dear. We can transform the ballroom into a pastoral setting with potted ferns and flowers. I wonder where we can find olive branches on such short notice? Oh, well, we shall do our best. I must find Charles. He must set the gardeners to work immediately. How shall I ever get him to wear one of those sheets? He will not like it at all, I fear." And on a tide of such reflections, she bustled from the room, leaving Miranda staring bemusedly after her.

It was not till long after tea that Miranda ventured forth from her room in search of diversion from her unrewarding thoughts. Quietly she slipped downstairs and through an empty saloon into a secluded rose garden, there to wander aimlessly, a thoughtful frown on her brow.

She had come to no conclusions about how best to get past the inevitable confrontation with the Duke of Eversley. She had thought simply to send the lock of hair in an envelope by one of the servants, then had dismissed the idea as craven. No. She must pay up face-to-face like a gentleman, and yet she had no wish to make it a public matter. She must contrive to meet Eversley away from the others, though how this was to be brought about without further damage to her already much tarnished reputation she had no clear notion. It would not do to send him a note inviting him to a clandestine meeting. No doubt he would see it as a further attempt to entrap a duke into matrimony. And she had no desire to bring more disgrace down upon dear Cousin Tess.

Oh, how had she gotten herself into such a coil? She, who had nothing but disdain for those who were addicted to gambling? And yet she could not deny the thrill she had felt as she swept along at a perilous pace, her skill and daring pitted against those of the noted nonpareil. And she had almost won, would have won had she anticipated Eversley's ploy and guarded against it. She began to suspect that she had more of her ne'er-do-well father's blood in her than she had previously thought as she acknowledged to herself that if she had it to do over again, she would still accept the abominable man's challenge, that indeed she yearned with all her heart for a rematch that she might teach him what a Waincourt was made of.

It was then that at least one of her difficulties resolved itself as suddenly a tall, elegant figure detached itself from the shadows beneath a grape arbor and strolled leisurely toward her. Miranda stiffened as she recognized the cause of all her most recent troubles. She dropped into a deep curtsy not lacking in grace despite its patent irony and rose to confront the duke with an absurdly pounding heart.

"Your Grace," she said, outwardly calm, and clasped her hands together before her to still their trembling.

"I see you are not one to tarry where a debt of honor is concerned," he drawled maddeningly, a gleam of laughter in those startlingly blue eyes. "An admirable trait. And how clever of you to follow me out here where no one might witness our transaction. You are a resourceful woman."

"I am nothing of the kind!" she retorted, then halted in confusion. "I mean I am, but not as you would imply." She blushed as the finely molded lips curled quizzically and could not resist a small gurgle of laughter at the masterful way in which he had trapped her into so foolish a statement. "You, my lord Duke, are incorrigible," she said ruefully. "Has no one ever got the better of you?"

A strange glitter lit the gaze he bent upon her.

"Not until I met you, my dear Miss Waincourt. But you seem destined to best me at every turn."

"I?" she questioned in obvious disbelief. "I have seen no sign of it. I fear your meaning escapes me, Your Grace."

"I am ruefully aware of that, my dear, but I am hopeful of one day amending that situation."

Her gaze fell away from his at this unexpected utterance and, pretending a sudden interest in the newly budding roses, she turned away to hide her mounting confusion at his unusually softened mood. Had she not known him better, she might have believed an offer was forthcoming, and unaccountably her pulse leaped at such a thought. And then she had herself in hand again, as she recalled the real motive behind his charming front. No doubt he referred to his failure to win the wager with Sir Charles, she thought with a sudden resurgence of the hurt and anger she had felt upon hearing his sardonic admission of culpability beyond the library door. Well, that was one wager he would never win, she vowed, and turned to meet his glance with cool disdain.

"But none of this is to the point, my lord Duke," she said haughtily. "The fact remains that I lost the race and now must make reparation for what I owe you. Unfortunately, I was not so resourceful as you have imagined me to be, and, *not* knowing you would be here, I failed to bring the—er—necessary instruments to—well—to..."

"You did not bring cutting shears with you, Miss Waincourt?" Eversley obligingly finished for her, thus rescuing her from her hopelessly convoluted sentence.

"Exactly so, Your Grace," she replied with admirable composure, though inwardly she seethed at the telltale twitch of the handsome lips.

"But I have not been so remiss, my dear Miss Waincourt." And with a mocking glance, he pulled a small pair of scissors from his coat pocket. "If you will allow me, I promise not to wreak undue havoc on your lovely hair. Just a small snip from the back should do admirably."

Miranda swallowed and obediently turned her back to him.

"Very well, Your Grace. I shall just have to trust you," she said stiffly and closed her eyes tightly as though in anticipation of a painful operation. Thus she did not see the grin of unholy amusement that lit his face, or the succeeding wave of tenderness as he fingered a fiery curl.

"I wish you may learn to trust me implicitly, my dear," he murmured meaningfully and severed the curl neatly from her head.

Miranda, who could not keep from wincing at the soft rasp of the blades, spun to face the duke with glittering eyes.

"Trust you, my lord Duke? I should never be so foolish. And now, if you will excuse me, I have other more pressing matters to attend."

"Another of your swains, no doubt," he observed, his glance narrowing speculatively on her flushed face.

"But of course," she replied airily, feeling suddenly flustered at finding him so near and not wanting him to see how perilously close she was to falling into a fit of the vapors. Really, she hardly knew herself anymore, she thought distractedly as she heard a worldly trill of laughter escape her lips. "I find that I am much sought after these days. Why, I never dreamed I should be so well amused at my cousin's house party. Aunt Agatha will be so pleased."

"Indeed?" he queried, and she shivered at the sudden hint of steel in the sleepy voice.

Driven by some perverse impulse to humiliate him as he had unwittingly humiliated her, she glanced coyly up at him out of the corner of her eye.

"Oh, yes," she simpered. "Why, she despaired utterly of my ever making a match, and here I find myself positively overwhelmed by the flattering attentions of three of the most eligible bachelors in the realm. I vow, I have seldom been better entertained."

If she had hoped to get a rise from him, she was not to be disappointed, for suddenly she found her arms imprisoned in his merciless grasp. She stared into icy blue eyes that froze her with their contempt, and fought the sudden weakness that pervaded her limbs.

"You little doxy," he growled between clenched teeth. "If it is a match you are after, why did you let me slip from your snare? You contrived so well, after all, to compromise yourself with me. Just what are you after?"

"A-after?" Miranda echoed, scarcely able to gather her scattered wits.

"Do not play the innocent miss with me, my dear. I know you for the scheming female you are. And you may be sure I shall not hesitate to make your true nature known to my two besotted friends.''

''And what, my lord Duke, may be my *true* nature?'' Miranda queried, her heart leaden within her breast.

''If not for an accident of birth, you, my dear, would undoubtedly have been a demirep, for behind that deceptively innocent façade there beats the scheming heart of a courtesan who will stop at nothing to ensnare any unwitting male who chances into her path. But for what purpose, I cannot help but wonder.''

He had ended with a sort of bewildered shake of his head, which, unbeknownst to the by now thoroughly incensed Miranda, was a reflection of the rending pain he had experienced at discovering she was apparently as false as all the others of her sex.

Miranda, beside herself with rage at his scathing condemnation of her character, leaped characteristically into the breach.

''But you need not wonder any longer, my lord Duke,'' she retorted witheringly. ''I am, after all, a confirmed spinster and man-hater. Perhaps it amuses me to lure unsuspecting members of the opposite sex into my coils. It is the favorite pastime of the famed Inconquerables, is it not? Why should I, a woman, be any different? Yet while you are hailed as a rake and courted all the more persistently for your alleged charms, I am sunk beneath reproach and relegated to the level of a doxy and a demirep. But perhaps it would be amusing to see whom I might bring up to scratch. Pulvney, perhaps? Or even Chomney? It is not given to every woman to win offers from the three Inconquerables in a single fortnight, and you, after all, have already succumbed to my wiles.''

"You shall soon catch cold at any such attempt, my dear,'' he drawled, releasing her as if he could no longer bear to touch her. "I advise you to give up so inadvisable a course of action and return to the safety of your brother's home. Believe me, you are not up to my weight in the sort of game you have chosen to play.''

"That remains to be seen, my lord Duke,'' she retorted with a toss of her head, then, fearful lest her trembling limbs should cease to support her, she briefly curtsied and fled with as much dignity as she could summon in her flustered state. Consequently, she did not see the duke bend to retrieve the coppery curl that had fallen unheeded to his feet. Nor did she know how long he stood staring after her, a curiously blank look in his eyes.

CHAPTER NINE

IT SEEMED, as she began preparations for the coming ball, that Lady Tess had succeeded in banishing her fears that soon she would be permanently exiled in shame to the provinces. Her cheeks glowed with becoming color and her lovely eyes sparkled with excitement as she attended to the hundred and one tasks inherent in such an undertaking. Her lilting voice could be heard issuing orders to the ranks of harried servants under her command, and the manor teemed with unrelenting activity that drove her fond husband to remark that at last his darling Tess had come into her own again. He had not liked the despondent droop to his wife's lovely mouth or the air of impending doom that she had worn immediately prior and subsequent to the scandalous race to which he had become an unwilling party. If it took the admittedly nerve-racking hustle and bustle of a ball to bring the color back to her face, then he was perfectly willing to suffer it for her sake.

Nor was he allowed to escape an active participation in transforming the ballroom into a suitable pastoral setting. Indeed, the indefatigable Tess kept them all hopping. Miranda she set to addressing invitations, while her cousin's three swains were assigned innumerable errands that took them all over the countryside. The earl and the marquess appeared to take all in stride, deriving no little amusement from Sir Charles's air of harried tolerance, and if they noticed Eversley's withdrawal behind a mask of studied ennui, they made no comment, attributing it perhaps to his well-known propensity to become bored at the first sign that he might be called upon to tax his energies for a cause with which he had little sympathy. At any rate, they could not deny that Eversley, as was ever the case, had pulled off a coup that could not be topped. For he had, in his inimitable way, provided the olive branches that the bothersome Tess had declared she simply must have if the ball were not to be a total failure. Indeed, he had caused to be delivered to her door a dozen live olive trees, all properly potted, as well as half a dozen fig trees, all of which earned him his hostess's undying affection and his own release from further assigned tasks.

As for Miranda, she had begun to display a marked loss of appetite and a tendency to become lachrymose at the least little upset. Indeed, she hardly knew herself anymore, she decided as she gazed with no little disgust at her pallid cheeks and shadowed eyes. Even Madame Tusseaud had been driven to take her to task after finding it necessary for the second time to take in the newly finished riding habit before Miranda had even had the chance to wear it, as well as the walking dress, the morning and evening gowns and the Grecian robe that had been made up earlier.

"Whatever has got into you, Miranda?" queried Lady Tess in sincere concern, as she studied her cousin's drooping figure beneath the loosely hanging ball gown that Madame Tusseaud was even then pinning up. "This is not at all like you."

"Is it not?" replied the young lady somewhat listlessly. "But then, I am not used to spending all day indoors. No doubt that is all that is wrong with me."

"But of course that must be it," Tess concluded brightly. "And I insist you take yourself off immediately Madame Tusseaud is finished with you. Now, now, no arguments. I shall rub along well enough without you. After all, everything is nearly in readiness, and you have worked like a Trojan. Jeremy and Chums are away to the village, I fear. And Evan has taken himself off to Lud only knows where. But perhaps you shall not mind riding by yourself. I see no need for a companion so long as you remain on the grounds. You are, after all, well able to take care of yourself."

Lady Tess was immediately awarded a bright smile for her thoughtfulness, and it was not long before Miranda, dressed to the nines in an emerald-green riding habit trimmed *à la militaire*, slipped unobtrusively from the house to the stable, her heart considerably lightened at the prospect of a brisk gallop on her beloved Aster.

Not wishing to encounter any of the other guests, particularly the masculine kind, Miranda headed her long-legged mare away from the road that led to the village and soon found herself out of sight of the house on the far side of a hill to the north of Applegarth. She rode with a lighthearted abandon she had not felt since leaving Groves, and it was not long before her cheeks were delicately tinged with healthy color and her eyes were bright with reflected enjoyment of the outdoors and her physical exertions. Thus it was perhaps not surprising that Eversley, coming unexpectedly upon her as he rounded a bend in the trail they both traversed, should stare in startled admiration at her lovely features.

"Oh!" Miranda gasped as she pulled Aster up just short of a collision, her pert riding hat with the upturned brim and the curling ostrich feather dyed to match her habit tumbling to the ground as the mare reared in protest. "Why is it that I must always be running into you, I wonder."

"An unkind fate indeed," feelingly murmured the duke with a curt bow that few could execute with such grace from the back of a restive steed. "I see that little has changed since our first unfortunate meeting," he added with a sardonic glance at the riding hat, which was perilously close to being trampled beneath the mare's hooves. "But at least this example of feminine headgear is more worthy of rescue than that other miserable excuse for a hat."

"I beg you will not trouble yourself, my lord Duke," Miranda said stiffly and made as if to swing down from her mount. She was halted by an ungentle hand about her wrist and ice-cold eyes that somehow took her breath away.

"Nevertheless, you will remain where you are while I play the gallant. It is the prerogative of the gentleman to retrieve a lady's fallen articles, and even in light of the possible equality of the sexes, I am not prepared to relinquish this small *convenance*. It gives one at least the illusion of civility, would you not agree?''

Before she could formulate a suitably scathing reply to his cynical observation, he had dismounted from the magnificent gray stallion that he bestrode and recovered the imperiled headgear.

"Madam," he intoned as he proffered the hat, then, to her obvious discomfort, remained staring up into her face, an arrested expression in his compelling gaze.

"Thank you, Your Grace," Miranda said, attempting to tug her property from his grasp. "And now if you will simply give me my hat, I shall trouble you no more."

"Have you been unwell, Miss Waincourt?" he asked abruptly. "You do not appear to be in your usual good looks."

"How chivalrous of you to point it out, my lord Duke," Miranda retorted dulcetly and was surprised to see a glint of humor lighten his somber expression. "I have been quite well, thank you."

"You do not look it. Has Tess been working you too hard on this damnable ball?"

"I beg your pardon, but if you insist on expressing yourself in such language, I see nothing for it but to ride on, notwithstanding the regrettable loss of my new hat."

"You have obviously lost weight, and there are shadows beneath your eyes, but your spirit is unimpaired, I see," he said with a satisfaction she found faintly disturbing. Surely he was not still bent on winning his bet with Sir Charles. If so, he was either the most obstinate man she had ever met or the greatest coxcomb. And yet she could not quite subdue a small shiver of delight that he might indeed be just the tiniest bit concerned for her health.

Immediately she quelled so disastrous a sentiment, calling to mind all the abominable things he had said to her at their last encounter. Unconsciously her head lifted, and she sat her horse a little straighter.

"I have perhaps grown a trifle wan from being inside too much," she said somewhat wistfully. "At home I was used to ride every day in all kinds of weather. I do miss it."

"And you are chafing, no doubt, to return to your beloved Groves, your three obstreperous siblings and the eccentric aunt who is desirous of marrying you off to the first eligible bachelor who offers," he said with a cynical quirk of an eyebrow.

"Oh, no," she disclaimed archly. "You misjudge Aunt Agatha if that is what you think. For I have already turned down my first two proposals of marriage. She realizes that I am extremely exacting and would no sooner expect me to wed in haste than she would expect me to purchase a stud for the brood mares without first examining his bloodlines."

She watched with a touching innocence the interesting wash of color rise to His Grace's face.

"Impudent baggage! How dare you compare me to one of your studs," he said with obvious feeling.

"And are not women constantly compared to horses? We are fillies to be tamed and nags to be beaten. Why, we are even displayed like prize brood mares for the highest bidder at the marriage mart of the elite, better known as Almack's. We are taught to parade and prance like the showiest of hacks. And before an offer is made, our pedigrees are checked to make certain we are of suitable lineage to bear our lord's offspring. Why, my lord, I can scarcely understand why you should find it distasteful to be compared to a prized stud,'' she finished with a limpid gaze from her emerald eyes. Then, finally wresting her hat from his grasp and placing it jauntily atop her coppery curls, she lifted the reins and sent her mount past him on the trail, her gurgle of laughter trailing behind her.

But she was not to escape so easily, she discovered as she became aware of the thunder of hooves in hot pursuit. She risked one quick glance over her shoulder and saw the duke's rangy gray stretched out in the long easy stride of the full-blooded Arabian. No wonder Sir Charles had been unable to resist temptation, she thought fleetingly. She would have found it difficult to turn down the chance of adding that bit of prime blood to her stables. Then she clapped heels to her long-limbed mare and was heading at breakneck speed down the narrow trail.

The track wound its way over gently rolling pastureland bordered on either side by thick hedgerows and was wide enough only for the occasional farm cart or two horses running abreast. Miranda, leaning low over her mount's neck, let the mare have her head. After her first brief glance back she had not dared to risk another, for the track was strange to her and she had no wish to risk injury to her mount. Even so, she knew the duke was gaining by the steady sound of hoofbeats coming up behind her. Ahead she spied a gate made of poles suspended between two beams and mentally judged its height at ten hands or better. Beyond, the trail stretched smoothly. She headed the mare straight for the gate, never slackening the pace. Flinging her heart over before her, the dainty mare took the gate easily, then obediently lengthened her stride as Miranda called to her. Aster responded with the smooth gait that had long before endeared her to her mistress. She might not be the stallion's match in a long run, but she had the heart of a champion, and Miranda knew how to call out the best in her.

No sooner had that thought entered Miranda's mind than disaster struck. A small dog, yapping furiously, bounded out into the track from a gap in the hedgerow. Aster shied violently and stumbled, her momentum carrying her to her knees. Miranda was flung head over heels from the mare's back and lay still, the breath knocked out of her. Her last conscious thought was of someone shouting her name and pounding to her side. Then with a sigh she fainted.

She awakened to the gentle touch of sensitive hands feeling for broken bones. With a barely suppressed moan, she opened her eyes to discover the duke kneeling over her, his face oddly white beneath his tan. And then she remembered.

"Aster!" she cried in a weak voice and struggled to sit up, but the duke pressed her gently down again.

"She's up and none the worse for wear," he said calmly, "which is more than I can say for you."

"Please. I want to see her," Miranda insisted, her eyes huge and pleading in her white face. For a moment their glances locked. Then he nodded briefly and placed a firm arm behind her shoulders.

"Easy. I don't think anything's broken, but there's no knowing about internal injuries," he said as he lifted her against his hard chest.

The mare stood close by with her head down. Miranda called softly to her and was heartened to see the tapered ears flick alertly forward. With a low whinny, the mare stepped daintily to her mistress's side to nuzzle the girl's cheek.

"Oh, Aster!" Miranda breathed as she flung her arms around the mare's neck. "I should have wanted to die if you had been lamed." She hugged the mare close for a moment before allowing Eversley to gently shoo Aster away again. Then she settled wearily against the broad shoulder conveniently placed behind her and glanced ruefully up into the heavy-lidded blue eyes.

"It appears that I am in your debt once again," she said with a small laugh. "It is really too absurd." Then she looked away again, feeling suddenly ridiculously shy.

He did not answer for a moment, and she became acutely aware of his arms wrapped protectively about her. She stirred restlessly and felt him loosen his hold on her.

"Do you think you can stand?" he said at last, his voice unwontedly husky. "You've a nasty bruise on your forehead, and you've probably scrambled what few wits you have, but you seem lucid enough."

"Oh, I've suffered worse falls and lived to tell of it," she quipped a little too brightly.

"No doubt. I begin to wonder how you ever managed to survive to womanhood."

"Quite handily until you came into my life," she replied a little tartly. She felt shaken and bruised far more than she was willing to admit, and she was hardly in any shape to match wits with the tiresome duke. "Since that moment, however, I seem to have become uncommonly prone to mishap," she added wearily.

"I might have known you would lay this at my doorstep. Yet I assure you I had nothing to do with the unfortunate appearance of that disreputable mongrel."

"I pray you will not be so ridiculous, my lord Duke. I am not such a gudgeon as to blame you for what happened. I wonder if it would be too much to ask that you help me from this less than dignified position. And then I should be pleased if you troubled yourself no further with me."

"You, Miss Waincourt, are undoubtedly the most hen-witted female of my rather extensive acquaintanceship if you think I am going to allow you to ride home unattended. Despite your total lack of proper female sensibilities, which should have sent you into a lengthy swoon, you are in no condition to ride out alone."

"I shall most certainly go into a swoon, Your Grace, if you do not cease to yammer at me," she countered waspishly, one hand going to her aching forehead.

She was startled at the sudden rumble of his laughter and glanced up in indignation at his apparent heartlessness, only to be rendered quite speechless by the warm light in his eyes as he gazed ruefully down at her.

"Shall you indeed, Miss Waincourt?" he queried softly. "Somehow I doubt it. You, my dear little termagant, could never be so missish." Then she watched fascinated as the laughter faded from his eyes to be replaced by a suddenly determined gleam.

"No," she murmured as his head lowered toward hers.

It was an oddly gentle kiss that sent her head spinning. And when at last he drew away, his face was strangely blurred in her vision.

"I wish you will not do that whenever I am the least bit under the weather," she remarked rather disjointedly. "I may indeed be a doxy and a demirep at heart, but I do object to your taking such license with me at your slightest whim. Besides, I cannot think it at all proper when I have yet to inform Pulvney of my decision."

She felt him stiffen and realized suddenly just what she had said.

"So. Jeremy has indeed come up to scratch, has he?" she heard him say as if from a great distance and wished with all her heart that the distracting ringing sensation that had unaccountably set up such a din when his lips touched hers would cease to sound so persistently in her ears. "And what is your decision, I wonder? A marquess, after all, is not so far removed from a duke, and poor Jeremy would likely prove putty in your capable hands. Are you to be a marchioness then, my dear?"

"Whether I am or not, I hardly see that it concerns you, my lord," Miranda evaded and, assisted by the seemingly preoccupied duke, climbed shakily to her feet.

Miranda was finding it difficult to think clearly and attributed her befuddlement to her fall from the horse. She was certain of one thing only: that she had gotten herself into deep water once again and must make her escape before she was utterly lost. She made to go over to her mare, but Eversley's hand closed inexorably about her wrist. She halted with her back to him and fought to hide the trembling of her limbs.

"Why Pulvney, Miss Waincourt?" he queried in a steely voice. "It cannot be his title or his fortune, for you had your chance at greater and turned them down."

In sudden anger at his unreasonable insistence that she was some loathsome, scheming creature, she swiveled to face him with her head held high.

"Oh, I *am* relieved that you do not regard me as a fortune hunter as well as a doxy," she applauded with the air of one who has been justly vindicated. It seemed, then, that she could not curb her wayward tongue as suddenly she gave vent to her hitherto bottled-up resentment for his many unkind aspersions on her character. "And since it appears that we must somehow determine my motives before I am to be allowed to return home, perhaps we should consider the possibility that I have fallen head over ears in love with Pulvney—just as on one particularly memorable occasion you advised me to do with *someone*, my lord Duke, indeed, with *anyone*—and now I see that you are right and I have been wrong to waste myself in the unproductive role of aunt." She paused, apparently to reflect, one finger pressed to her lips. "But no. That will not do at all, will it? For I am, alas, a 'man-hater' and an 'avowed spinster.' Oh, dear.'' She shrugged prettily. ''Apparently there is no satisfactory explanation. I am sorry, but apparently I shall simply have to remain an enigma.''

''Very prettily done, my dear,'' observed the duke with a speculative gleam in his eyes. ''But that is the second time you have referred to yourself as a 'man-hater' and an 'avowed spinster.' Do they have some special significance for you, Miss Waincourt?''

''Surely I cannot be misinformed,'' she rejoined in apparent innocence oddly at variance with the emerald flash of her eyes. ''That is what you have called me, is it not? And I cannot help but point out, Your Grace, the apparent inconsistencies in your various evaluations of my character. Can I possibly be both a 'confirmed spinster' and a 'doxy'? But then, that is, of course, the answer! A spinster who hated men might very likely delight in luring her helpless prey on with the skills of a Cyprian only to humiliate him in the end by dashing his expectations. And what a brilliant scheme! But you have found me out, haven't you, my lord Duke? I congratulate you on your sagacity and advise you to inform Pulvney with all haste of your findings,'' Miranda finished bitterly, then abruptly averted her face that he should not see the sudden glimmer of tears in her eyes.

''Oh, yes,'' she added in a muffled voice. ''Go and warn him, but it will little serve you. For I have decided in the end, you see, to accept him, thus putting your theory to the lie!''

CHAPTER TEN

THE RIDE BACK to Applegarth was accomplished in taut silence. Miranda, suffering now from a throbbing headache as well as numerous aches and bruises, was made to feel even more miserable by the contemplation of her ill-considered declaration that she would have Pulvney. Clearly she must be mad to have done anything so foolish. Pointedly she ignored the instigator of her most recent headlong plunge into deep waters as they topped the low rise above Applegarth and headed down the bridle path toward the stables. Never until the irksome duke had disastrously intruded into her life had anyone been able to send her so thoroughly into the boughs as to make her utterly forget herself. She had reacted with disastrous results to his barbed accusations and made a mull of everything. But at least Aunt Agatha would be in alt over her coming nuptials, she mused fatalistically and tried not to imagine poor Pulvney's horror at having to welcome into his home two grubby schoolboys, her eccentric Aunt Agatha and one small female with a voracius billy goat. It really was too absurd. It was, in fact, out of the question.

She could see nothing for it but that she must just give the proof of the duke's odious pudding and inform the marquess immediately of her intention to remain in the single state. Poor Tess! No doubt she would take it hard when it became known her disreputable cousin had once again sunk herself beneath reproach, for she was quite positive that once she had turned down Pulvney's offer, Eversley would not hesitate to make good his threat to expose Miranda to his two friends as a totally unscrupulous female whose sole purpose in life was to ensnare any poor unsuspecting bachelor who came her way. As if she could have done, she thought incredulously. Obviously the man was suffering from delusions, for despite her admittedly improved appearance, she was scarcely possessed of the alluring charms of a Circe.

Oh, however had she got herself into such an idiotish bumble broth? she wondered irritably as she pulled Aster up before the stable. Nor was her temper noticeably improved when she looked suddenly down into glittering blue eyes and discovered the insufferable Duke of Eversley waiting to help her dismount.

"You seem uncommonly distracted, Miss Waincourt," murmured His Grace frostily and placed strong hands about her slender waist to lift her down from the saddle. "I do hope you are not having second thoughts, for if I am not mistaken, that is your intended approaching even now. How I should dislike to see poor Pulvney in the lurch," he added significantly.

Stifling an indignant gasp, Miranda glanced quickly up to behold the tall marquess sauntering toward them. It needed only this, she thought, and in morbid fascination watched his smile fade, to be replaced by

a quick expression of astonished concern as he too.
her considerably battered black beaver hat with the
curled-up brim, the ostrich feather drooping at a disreputable angle over one eye and her emerald-green
riding habit trimmed *à la militaire* looking as if it had
been through a recent battle.

"My dear Miss Waincourt!" he exclaimed, his usual
languid drawl in abeyance, and quickened his pace.
"What has happened? Are you all right?"

"No need to get into a quake, Jeremy," interjected
the duke ironically. "Your betrothed has had a bit of
a fall, but she assures me she has suffered worse and
lived to tell of it."

Miranda awarded the odious duke a single fulmi-
nating glance.

"I beg your pardon?" queried Pulvney, brought
suddenly to a jolting halt. His pale blue eyes probed,
regarded the patently bored features of his oldest
friend, then swept to the lady's lovely countenance,
which appeared suddenly and alarmingly devoid of all
color. He stared entranced into emerald-green eyes
that seemed to flash sparks of glittering anger, and
thought how very beautiful she was. The thought
briefly came to him that something other than his beloved's apparent mishap was amiss, when at last he
was struck by the full significance of the duke's cryptic remark.

"Betrothed?" he questioned slowly, struggling to
make sense of a situation that seemed fraught with
undercurrents of meaning beyond his immediate
comprehension. "What does this mean, Miss Waincourt?"

"I fear His Grace has spoken out of turn, m'lord. This is hardly the time or place to speak of such a delicate matter," Miranda said in a last desperate attempt to put off the inevitable, then mentally gnashed her teeth as it became obvious that His Grace of Eversley was not to be satisfied with anything short of a public declaration of her intent.

"Nonsense, Miss Waincourt," he said cuttingly. "Surely there is little point in keeping Pulvney hanging. The *lady* has decided to accept your offer, Jeremy. And I wish you luck with your future bride. You will no doubt need it," he finished and with a curt bow wheeled to stalk deliberately away from the happy couple.

The Marquess of Pulvney turned to study Miranda with his customary deliberation. Somehow his love had not the look of one who had just decided to accept the man of her dreams. Indeed, she appeared more in the frame of mind to commit murder as she gazed after the tall form of his friend.

"Miss Waincourt?" he questioned uncertainly. "Miranda? Is what Eversley said the truth? Have you decided to make me the happiest man in the world by becoming my wife?"

Miranda seemed suddenly jolted back to an awareness of his presence, he noted ruefully and wondered what had occurred that morning between the duke and his elusive love. She evinced all the signs of one who labored beneath a heavy burden, and instinctively he knew she was about to deny Eversley's heated assertion. He knew as well that she did not love him, but it was rare that members of his class married out of love. The significant difference was that he loved her.

He had come late in life to such a state of mind, for he was eight and thirty, and he had not known if he could ever adapt his style of living to include a wife. Indeed, had he never met Miranda, he no doubt would have been content to remain a bachelor all his days. For he was a man who preferred an undemanding, unfettered existence. Nor had the urge to beget an heir to the title and his considerable fortune moved him to offer for this strangely beguiling young woman. He did not like children, for they tended to cut up one's tranquillity. Furthermore, he was not displeased with the notion that his cousin would inherit. The lad was capable and already had fathered a brood of young hopefuls to carry on the Bannington name. No. Rather, it was the unexpected discovery that he was comfortable with Miss Waincourt, who demonstrated a pleasing tolerance for his rather ponderous nature. For while he was not lacking in sagacity, he had formed the habit of careful cogitation before declaring himself on any matter, with the result that many thought him a slow top. But not Miss Waincourt, who seemed to understand his deliberative inclination and to appreciate his droll sense of humor. In short, while he was quite sure he could continue in his customary tranquillity should she choose not to wed him, he thought that perhaps his life would seem rather empty without her.

Thus, determined to win her if he could, he did not choose to press her at a time when she was certain to deny his suit. It behooved him to leave matters as they were, on the slim chance that she would grow used to the idea of becoming his wife. Nor did he doubt that it weighed in his favor that she seemed at least on the surface committed to him, for the longer she waited to cry off, the harder it would become.

Consequently, he solicitously took her arm and began to stroll leisurely toward the manor.

"Never mind, my dear," he said, patting her hand sympathetically. "You are in no condition to contemplate serious matters at this time. We shall talk later, after you have rested."

Miranda, who did not feel at all able to deal with anything more exacting than a long soak in a hot bath, awarded him a grateful smile and, leaning on his arm, allowed him to lead her to the house.

MIRANDA PACED FURIOUSLY back and forth across the Aubusson carpet that bedecked the hard wood floor of her bedchamber. She had spent a sleepless night mulling over her latest dilemma and had come to only two conclusions regarding her plight. First and foremost, she must somehow break off the engagement with Pulvney before he made it public at the ball, which was to be held that very evening. And second, she was quite sure she had never detested anyone quite so much as she detested the Duke of Eversley. That neither conclusion made her feel any the better she refused to contemplate. Indeed, she felt stiff and sore, which she attributed quite reasonably to her fall from Aster, but she was also experiencing a bewildering turmoil of emotions fluctuating from a distressing urge to break things to an unwonted tendency to burst suddenly into tears, which she could not explain at all.

"Oh, the devil fly away with all men!" she abruptly exclaimed to the room in general and then bit her lip to still its sudden trembling. No doubt she would have succumbed to a threatening fit of the vapors had not a light rap, followed by her cousin's blithe entrance into her chamber, forced her to assume a calm façade.

"Miranda, whatever are you doing up here? We have already finished with tea and still you have not shown yourself. Why, my dear! What is the matter? You look sadly pulled. Do not say you are coming down with something, for I shall never stand for it. You simply cannot cry off from the ball."

For a moment Miranda was sorely tempted to do just that, but one look at her cousin's expression of alarm was enough to quell such a craven thought. She could not use Tess so badly. No, she would just have to make the best of things.

"No, no. It's nothing," she said instead. "I'm still a trifle shaken up from my absurd fall yesterday and I'm afraid I didn't sleep all that well last night. But I shall be fine after a nap."

"But of course you will," the indomitable Tess replied, perceptibly brightening. "Though how you ever came to such a mishap I shall never understand, for I have never seen anyone so well as you on a horse. But never mind that for now. I look to you to aid me in my hour of travail, for I must tell you Charles has proved unaccountably pig-headed. He insists he will not make such a fool of himself as to run about half-naked in a

sheet and stands upon his right as host not to appear
in costume. Whatever shall I do? For you must understand that I had particularly looked forward to
wearing a Grecian robe and doing my hair *à la Méduse*. And so I have told him. But though he says he
would do anything for me, he will not do this one little thing. Whatever shall I do, Miranda?''

Miranda could not help the sudden bubble of
laughter that rose to her throat at the sight of Tess's
tragic pose. Poor Sir Charles! He would have a sad
time of it for his unexpected firmness on this matter of
his dignity.

"Oh, you may well laugh, cousin," Lady Tess
complained. "But I do indeed find myself in the lurch.
For you must know I was never bookish. And I still
haven't the slightest idea what personage would best
suit me. I depend utterly on you to tell me how I must
go on."

"But, my dear hen-witted cousin," rejoined Miranda with a devil lurking in her green eyes, "there is
only one who is particularly suited to your needs. You
must go as Aphrodite, the goddess of beauty and love.
And I shall be Atalanta, the virgin huntress," she
added with a look that caused Tess suddenly to sit up
in renewed alarm.

"I do see that I might indeed suit as Aphrodite,"
she said ingenuously, "for I have ever been of a romantical nature. But why should you choose this virgin huntress?"

"Because Atalanta swore never to submit to any
man—indeed, never to marry. And so, too, have I,"
Miranda answered with a rather grim smile. "I shall

need a buckle of polished gold and an ivory quiver. And in my hand I shall carry a bow. Oh, it is too perfect."

Tess regarded her tall, slender cousin in some dismay. No doubt the girl could play the role of virgin huntress admirably, for she had rather the look of an Amazon just then with her eyes flashing and her jaw set with such stern resolution. She was positively daunting! And yet Lady Tess could not like the part about vowing never to marry. It boded ill for her own plans for the girl. And just when everything was looking so promising, too!

"She sounds a queer sort of creature," Tess could not help but remark with a dubious lift of one lovely eyebrow. "And did no enterprising young man ever overcome her aversion to matrimony?"

"Well, yes, as a matter of fact one eventually did," Miranda reluctantly answered. "But only because Aphrodite helped to trick her. But that is not to the point. Atalanta will suit me very well, I've no doubt," she finished with a peculiar gleam in her eye. "For this is one race in which I shall *not* be bested."

Then Miranda refused to say another word about the virgin huntress, turning the subject instead to a discussion of Tess's proposed costume.

"You will need an embroidered girdle, which was called a cestus, and which had the power of inspiring love. And you must carry a swan or a dove and wear rose and myrtle, since these were always associated with Aphrodite."

"Oh, dear," fluttered the aspiring goddess of beauty and love, more than a little daunted at such a prospect. "I cannot think it will be at all comfortable to be forever carrying around a swan. However should I go on, Miranda? The thing would be forever pecking at me and I do not think anyone, not even Charles, would be moved to partner me in a waltz with such a creature beneath my arm. Besides which, I cannot think a swan's manners could be at all nice in polite company. No doubt it would think nothing of soiling my gown. And that would not do at all."

"N-no doubt you are in the right of it." Miranda choked, much struck by her cousin's commonsensical approach to the matter. "Possibly a mere representation of a swan will suit, however."

"That would be much better," Tess rejoined quite seriously, then, catching sight of the gleam of mirth in Miranda's eyes, began to giggle. "Oh, dear," she gasped. "What an utter gudgeon I am. I shall simply have to take myself off before I disgrace myself further. Do get some rest, my dear. You must not have circles beneath your eyes tonight. They are most unflattering as a rule, and Spenser would never forgive you, you know."

"Indeed, she has made her feelings quite plain in the past. But in this instance I'm afraid I shall just have to disappoint her. It seems I shall have to see to a costume after all."

"Oh, never mind that. I can find all that you will need. A gold buckle will not be difficult, and I know there is a bow in the attic. Of course, an ivory quiver may prove somewhat troublesome, but Spenser will help me to contrive something for you. You lie down on your bed and trust me."

Miranda was grateful to do just as her cousin commanded her, for indeed she was feeling worn to the nub after her sleepless night. Thus it was not long before she slumbered peacefully in her bed, oblivious to the fact that her modern-day Aphrodite was up to her old tricks again.

Lady Tess, upon leaving her cousin, made straightway for Sir Charles's book room, a chamber that as a rule she had little need to visit.

"Now, how do you suppose one goes about finding such a thing?" she muttered, quite distracted by the sheer number of volumes confronting her. Then she started violently as a lazy drawl sounded from behind her. With a gasp, she wheeled to discover the Duke of Eversley regarding her with obvious amusement from his seat in the caffoy-covered wing chair before the fireplace. She noticed fleetingly that he was rather carelessly attired in buff riding breeches and a dark blue coat of superfine, a scarf tied negligently about his neck in lieu of a neckcloth. His normally indecently shining Hessians were dulled by a layer of dust, evidence of a recent ride, and his black hair tumbled about his head in unusual disarray. A half-empty bottle of port and a full glass would seem to indicate that His Grace had been making indentures, mused the lady with sudden interest, for it was never Evan's normal practice to imbibe much before the fashionable hour of five. Indeed, it appeared the duke was in a somber mood.

"Perhaps were you to tell me what you are looking for, I might be of some assistance," he was saying as he rose languorously to his feet, his lips curved in the engaging grin he reserved for his intimate friends.

"Evan!" exclaimed the lady, one dainty hand pressed to her bosom. "You startled me out of a year's growth. How dare you sneak up on me like that!"

"But I protest, darling Tess. I did not sneak. I was merely perusing the newspaper in this chair when I heard you enter and mumble something about wishing to find something."

"Oh, how odious of you." She giggled. "I'll have you know I never mumble." Then she pursed her lips thoughtfully and turned the full force of her gaze upon His Grace, who groaned inwardly at what he perceived to be her meddlesome look. "But never mind. I forgive you. And actually, you can be of use to me."

"Enough, Tess," Eversley said, suddenly devoid of all humor, and raised one hand as if to ward her off. "You know I will not play the dupe in your matchmaking schemes. Besides, the bird is fairly caught. And don't say you knew nothing of your cousin's betrothal to Pulvney, for I shan't believe you. It has been your intention all along to see one of the Inconquerables brought low, has it not?"

"Pulvney?" exclaimed Lady Tess, judiciously ignoring the latter part of his speech. "You cannot mean Jeremy has indeed come up to scratch? But I promise Miranda never told me. And it makes no sense, for if you must know, I have just left her and she seemed as determined as ever to remain unattached, for why else should she choose such a queer character as this virgin huntress to impersonate at the ball?"

"Virgin huntress?" the duke quizzed, one dark eyebrow arching.

"Yes, yes. Atlantis or Atlas or some such thing. It has slipped my mind now and it is all your fault. And now I shan't be able to discover who it was who in the end won her hand or how Aphrodite managed it. It really is too bad of you, Evan."

"It was no doubt Atalanta, gudgeon," said the duke with an arrested air. "And Hippomenes who won her."

"Then you do know the tale and you will tell it to me. For Miranda would not. And I would rather not be bothered with going through all these monstrous books. It would be sure to give me a headache, and you simply could not wish for that, now could you?"

"Heaven forbid, dearest Tess. I should be sunk beneath reproach to desire any such thing."

"Oh, do stop bamming me, Evan," Tess returned with a moue of mock displeasure at his teasing. "I simply must know how Aphrodite tricked her."

"She helped Hippomenes beat Atalanta in a foot race, my dear. How, I wonder, would that aid you in your endless plotting?"

"In a foot race?" Tess echoed blankly. "Whatever can you mean?"

"Simply that Atalanta was promised to wed any man who could beat her in a foot race," replied the duke sardonically, but the blue eyes beneath the drooping lids appeared to glitter with less than his usual indifference, Tess noted with satisfaction. "Those whom she beat were put to death. Consequently, Hippomenes, who had unaccountably become infatuated with the girl but who obviously was rather wiser than his unfortunate predecessors, asked for Aphrodite's aid. The goddess of love obliged him by giving him three golden apples. These he dropped one at a time as he ran against his love. Because she stopped to retrieve each of the three apples, Hippomenes won the race and in the end experienced the dubious satisfaction of wedding his fair Atalanta. Now tell me, dearest Tess. How do you plan to use this odd piece of trivia, and against what poor soul?"

"Must you always be so cynical, Evan?" Lady Tess demanded with a charming pucker of her lovely brow. "Whatever am I to do with you?"

"Might I suggest that there is little you can do with me?" he countered acerbically. "And moreover, my lovely little ninnyhammer, that I wish devoutly that you will cease to try?"

"Oh dear," was Lady Tess's unruffled rejoinder, "you *are* in a nasty mood. But since we can never agree on that subject, I see little point in discussing it. What's more to the point is that this was not at all what I expected. I hardly see how such a tale can be of any use to me whatsoever. Really, I simply cannot understand Miranda. She was never used to be so changeable. Yet since she has arrived here, she has become utterly unpredictable."

"Indeed?" queried the duke, a look of profound boredom beginning to descend over his handsome features.

"That idiotish carriage race, for example," Lady Tess continued, apparently oblivious to the duke's drastically altered mood. "One moment I was quite sure I had induced her to cry off. I know I saw her coming toward the library soon after our little talk. Indeed, I watched her pause just outside the door, her hand raised as though she might knock. And then suddenly she went quite white and dashed on up the stairs. After that there was no dissuading her. And now you say she has agreed to marry Jeremy when she has just made it quite clear to me she means to do no such thing. It is simply beyond all understanding.''

The duke, who had apparently become even more deeply sunk into an advanced state of ennui, regarded the bewildered Lady Tess from under drooping eyelids.

''Quite so,'' he drawled and languidly brought forth an exquisite enameled snuffbox. Flipping the lid open with his thumb, he took a pinch of his favorite mixture and inhaled it, then, snapping closed the lid, replaced the box before continuing in tones of polite interest, ''And just when did this episode before the library door occur, I wonder?''

''Oh, I don't know. Shortly after our dear Lady Horton finally deigned to descend for her breakfast, I should think,'' Tess answered distractedly. ''Around eleven, I dare say. What possible difference could it make?''

''Probably none. I was just curious. And now I believe I must leave you to contemplate your incomprehensible cousin on your own. I do think I feel a nap coming on.''

This observation was greeted with what sounded suspiciously like a very unladylike snort from Lady Tess.

"I am sorry to have fatigued Your Grace," she said, dimpling naughtily, then suddenly frowned. "We will see you at the ball tonight, Evan?" she asked in ominous tones. "I shouldn't like to think you will be too fatigued to attend."

The duke's lips curved in the sardonic grin that effectively hid his inner thoughts and bowed courteously over the lady's hand.

"I shouldn't dream of missing seeing you attired as Aphrodite," he answered smoothly. "You may be sure that I shall be there."

"I am never sure of anything where you are concerned—which is just as you intend. But however did you know I was to go as Aphrodite when I only just decided upon it a few minutes ago myself?"

"But it is impossible that you should go as anyone else, my darling Tess." He laughed and turned to saunter leisurely toward the door.

"That is just what Miranda said," she called in perplexity after his retreating back.

He paused before stepping into the hallway and turned to regard her with a hint of amusement.

"Then you cannot doubt it, can you, my dear?"

Then he was gone, and Tess had begun to chuckle softly.

"You know me so well, dearest friend," she murmured with an air of great satisfaction. "And yet it would seem to me that you have fairly swallowed the bait."

Suddenly Lady Tess was looking forward to her ball with a deal more optimism than she had previously thought possible.

CHAPTER ELEVEN

"OH, MISS!" exclaimed Miranda's abigail, clasping her hands together before her in rapt admiration. "You be as lovely as a fairy princess!"

Miranda, eyeing herself critically in the mirror, could not deny that the simple Grecian robe seemed particularly suited to her, though, considering her generous inches, perhaps "fairy princess" was coming it a bit strong. The lustrous ivory linen, clasped at one shoulder with Tess's borrowed golden buckle and allowed to fall in soft, alluring folds to her sandaled feet, transformed her from an overly tall, rather gawky girl into a slender, willowy goddess. Even her hair, which had been Miranda's despair before coming to Applegarth and Cousin Tess's ingenious abigail, was subtly elegant. Indeed, she hardly recognized in this lovely creature, with the coppery tresses parted in the middle and clustering in wispy curls about the regal head *à la Titus*, the spinsterish hoyden of only a few days earlier.

Would the torpid duke think her fetching as the demigoddess Atalanta? she could not help wondering, upon which her eyes flashed emerald sparks. His Grace had left little doubt as to what he thought of her. Demirep and doxy indeed! Oh, the coxcomb! He

deserved to be hung, drawn, and quartered for such
abuse. That he should even for one moment believe
she was the deceitful, scheming wretch he had accused her of being was beyond the bounds of all decency. If only she were a man that she might call him
to account for his insult to her! But she was not a man.
She was a woman, but a woman who cared not one
whit what the odious duke might think of her, she told
herself and firmly adjusted the child's quiver covered
in ivory satin held to her back with gold cord. Tonight she would be the virgin huntress who had sworn
never to bow to any man. And even if on the morrow
she must be only Miranda Waincourt on her way home
to Groves, this night at least she meant to have the
time of her life.

So saying to herself, she picked up the strung bow
wrapped in satin ribbon to match the quiver, tossed
her coppery curls in a final gesture of determination,
and strode firmly from her bedchamber to join the
merriment already in progress in the ballroom below.

"Miranda! Where have you been?" scolded a
dainty manifestation of the goddess of love and beauty
standing in the doorway to greet the arriving guests.
"The music has already started."

"Tess! You look marvelous," Miranda gurgled,
taking in the vision of her cousin draped in white sarcenet, her Grecian curls crowned fetchingly with a
garland of roses intertwined with myrtle leaves. Having discarded the notion of the cumbersome swan, this
commonsensical Aphrodite wore a white-satin dove
bound with a ribbon about her wrist, and around her
waist a lovely embroidered girdle shot with gold.

"Never mind me," Tess whispered in a quick aside, then smiled and nodded graciously at an improbable Cupid graced with wings and weighing a good three hundred pounds. "Lud, I begin to see I was right not to insist that Charles make a ninny of himself," she giggled naughtily, apparently having forgotten that it was the baronet's adamant resolution to forgo the indignity of appearing in a sheet. But to Miranda's discomfiture, the determined Tess returned immediately to the subject of her protégée's late arrival.

"I have been in a pother thinking you had in the end decided to cry off. But I forgive you, for you look positively elegant, Miranda. And, after all, it may turn out for the best when one considers that two of our Inconquerables appear to be on tenterhooks over your elusiveness."

"Only two?" queried Miranda with a wry grin, thinking that the duke had had time enough to blacken her name and reputation and bring the whole county down on her with tar and feathers.

"Well, one can never tell what Eversley is thinking behind those sleepy eyes of his. But that is not to the point, for His Grace has not deigned to make his appearance yet. Nor do I look for him much before eleven, and then no doubt he will honor us with a generous twenty minutes of his precious time before retiring. However, even so brief a visit will crown the ball a success, which is as much as any hostess can hope for from the nonpareil. No, I don't think you can depend on Eversley to show marked interest in any of the single females present. It has never been his practice to encourage expectations he has no intention of fulfilling.''

But even as Tess spoke, Miranda looked up with an inexplicable fluttering of her heart to see the tall figure of the duke entering the ballroom.

He was easily the most striking figure in the mélange of Zeuses, Poseidons, Apollos and Cupids, she mused, taking in at a glance his masculine form garbed in an authentic reproduction of the Ionic chiton belted at the lean waist with a leather girdle. The short folds of a chlamys draped from the powerful shoulders, leaving his arms free. Miranda stifled an indignant gasp as she beheld, suspended from his belt in a net scrip, three golden apples.

"Late as usual, Evan," Tess chided as the duke bowed languorously over her dainty hand. "I had nearly given up on you."

"Can you have so little faith, fair Aphrodite?" drawled the duke lazily, his lips curved in a faint, sardonic smile. "But, as you see, I have kept my word." Then he turned to sweep Miranda with a careless glance. "Ah, Atalanta, is it not?" he queried, the blue eyes beneath the drooping eyelids mocking. "Somehow I should have thought Pandora with her bridal dowry more appropriate than the virgin huntress."

"Indeed, Your Grace?" rejoined Miranda in dulcet tones. "No doubt I am sorry to disappoint you. And yet I cannot help but wonder at your own choice of Hippomenes. Tell me, did you, like your classical counterpart, envoke the aid of Aphrodite, my lord Duke?" she ended, her emerald glance accusingly fixed on Lady Tess.

"Oh, dear," murmured the scheming goddess of love, dimpling in charming confusion. "I fear I did let slip to Evan your choice of costumes. But indeed, Miranda, I only meant to save myself the trouble of poring through all those books to discover what you yourself would not tell me. 'Tis your own fault for arousing my curiosity, only to leave me dangling. Evan was kind enough to finish the tale."

"No doubt," Miranda observed dryly. "And yet that still does not explain why his grace should choose to come as Atalanta's bridegroom."

Lady Tess, perceiving that the two whom she still entertained the fondest hopes of seeing united appeared on the verge of coming to blows, teasingly tapped Eversley on the wrist with her ivory fan.

"Now you have got me in the suds, Evan," she said, dimpling impishly, "I charge you to get me out again. You can explain everything while you and Miranda dance the waltz."

For a moment the mortal goddess of love feared she had gone too far as she watched the duke's eyebrow arch imperiously. But then the ghost of a smile touched his lips at the sight of the willowy Atalanta eyeing him with cool disdain. Why, the chit was daring him to show craven! he thought and determined that she should be shown the folly of her chosen path to iniquity.

"Miss Waincourt?" he murmured, bowing with easy grace. "Would you do me the honor?"

Miranda favored the duke with a suspicious glance, for she had been quite sure he had been about to refuse her cousin's unwelcome suggestion. Oh, how she would like to give the irksome nobleman the cut direct! But the lazy blue eyes seemed to challenge her to do just that. Well, she would show him she was never one to be fainthearted.

"My lord." She nodded graciously and allowed herself to be led onto the floor.

Miranda, whose sole experience with the new, undeniably controversial dance form had been to serve as a practice partner for her graceless younger brother Kit, had never dreamed that dancing in the arms of a man could be like soaring blissfully on a summer's breeze, or like participating in some sublime communication impossible with mere words, or like... But then her whimsical flight of fancy suffered a sudden, violent check, as the duke's sardonic drawl obtruded into her befuddled thoughts.

"I would not have you laboring under any false illusions, my dear Miss Waincourt," he murmured silkily into her ear. "Not as Atalanta's ill-fated bridegroom, surely, but as the only man to beat the avowed spinster at her own game, Hippomenes would seem a propitious choice, do you not agree?"

Miranda, unable to suppress a small gasp of outrage, stiffened, nearly losing the step. The gall of the man! She was quite sure she had never detested anyone quite so thoroughly. Determined, nonetheless, that he should not have the satisfaction of seeing her once again in the boughs, Miranda lifted limpid green eyes and smiled sweetly.

"Hardly, my lord Duke," she simpered, fluttering her luxurious eyelashes coquettishly up at him. "For one of your avowed sentiments I should have thought Narcissus far more apropros.''

''Quite so,'' agreed the duke with an appreciative gleam in his disturbing eyes. ''But what would you? Perhaps you would prefer that I present Aphrodite's golden apples to Pulvney. No doubt *he* will have need of them should he not see you for what you are—a scheming little trollop with a heart of stone.''

''Oh!'' Miranda breathed, abandoning all pretense of congeniality. ''You may dispose of them howsoever you will, I am sure,'' she said in an icy rage and wished she dared to tell him *exactly* what he could do with his absurd golden apples. ''I ask only that I never again have to suffer your vile insults. Pray do us both a favor and never speak to me again!'' With a last scathing glance, Miranda wheeled and swept haughtily into the midst of the swirling melee of dancers, leaving the duke standing, white-faced and glaring after her.

Thinking only to remove herself as far and as quickly from the detestable duke as was possible, Miranda in her hurry nearly collided with the Earl of Chomney, who, after one look at the vision of outraged femininity, instantly led her from the floor.

''Oh, my lord!'' she gasped and pressed a hand to her still-thumping heart. Grateful to have encountered a friendly face amid the sea of gaping strangers, Miranda awarded the earl a melting look.

''Miss Waincourt—Miranda, my dear. You seem overset. How may I be of service?''

''Please, just stay with me for a moment,'' replied Miranda, still shaking with rage. Then suddenly she giggled a trifle hysterically as she became fully aware of Chomney uncomfortably swathed in a sheet and hugging to his nearly bare chest a hefty three-foot-tall figurine of a voluptuously endowed young maiden about which he had chastely draped a white linen shawl. She saw in further mirthful amazement that jewels adorned the maiden's sculpted neck and upraised arm and a wreath of flowers her ceramic head.

"Whatever can you be doing with *that*?" she gurgled and went off into new paroxysms of laughter at the sight of the earl's aristocratic eyebrow shooting upward in pained dismay.

"Come now, Miss Waincourt. Surely you of all people must understand the significance of the statuette in my disguise," he replied in injured accents, but Miranda saw the ever-present twinkle in the gray eyes and was not fooled.

"Oh, then I am to guess your identity from the figurine," she said and made a show of raising a forefinger to pursed lips as though in deep cogitation. And, indeed, she was hard pressed for a time to resolve the riddle, enough so, in fact, that she did not notice the earl's twinkle of amusement vanish, to be replaced by a sudden gleam of enlightenment as he gazed upon her lovely, animated countenance.

"But of course! How clever you are!" she cried presently, her emerald eyes leaping with amused triumph to his face. "You are Pygmalion and that is Galatea, your idealized perfect mate."

But the earl was staring at her so strangely that she thought perhaps he must suddenly have taken ill.

"My lord?" she queried in some alarm. "Is something wrong?"

Chomney appeared mentally to shake himself.

"No, no. Forgive me. I'm afraid I am quite distracted tonight by as lovely a goddess as it has been my privilege to behold. Miss Waincourt, would you allow me the honor of dancing with you?"

"Oh, dear." Miranda blushed, reminded of her quarrel with the thoroughly odious duke. "I'm afraid I have behaved rather badly and shall no doubt discover myself once again quite persona non grata. I must tell you I have just left His Grace of Eversley in the lurch in the middle of the dance floor."

A flicker of astonishment passed briefly over the earl's urbane features. Had the invincible lothario then met his match at last? he marveled, gazing with ever-greater interest at this surprising beauty's troubled countenance.

"Nonsense," said the earl, laughing. "No doubt Evan got just what was due him. However, it is imperative that you do not buckle now. You will behave as though nothing untoward has occurred, beginning with your triumphant return to the scene of battle on my arm."

Thus saying, he heartlessly abandoned in one of the potted olive trees placed cunningly about the ballroom the idealized ceramic version of his perfect mate and swung the flesh-and-blood Miranda out onto the dance floor.

The Earl of Chomney, she discovered, was as accomplished on his feet as he was at repartee. In no time she had so far forgotten herself as to relax within the unfamiliar circle of his arm, her steps flowing easily with her partner's and her laughter gurgling deliciously as he entertained her with his ever-charming wit. All too soon, it seemed, the dance had come to an end, and Chomney was leading her from the floor.

"Will you save me the supper dance, my lovely Atalanta?" he said as he seated her next to Miss Marian Horton. "There is something I wish most particularly to discuss with you."

"I am sorry, my lord, but Pulvney is to take me in to supper. Perhaps the one after that?"

So agreeing, the earl bowed and took his leave of her, whereupon Miranda was immediately set upon by Sir Charles's vivacious young cousin, who made a charming Polyxena to her betrothed's Achilles.

"Isn't everything simply wonderful?" bubbled the girl with an exuberance in sharp contrast to the assumed world-weariness of most of her contemporaries. "I've never been to a masquerade ball before. I daresay Cousin Tess has outdone herself with this one."

Miranda had drawn a breath to answer that she was as little experienced in such matters as was her young friend, when she was startled by the girl's sudden exclamatory "Oh!" uttered in accents of awe.

"Isn't that Eversley with Helen of Troy?" Marian asked conspiratorially. "How well they look together! I wonder who she is."

Miranda heard little more of the girl's chatter. Indeed, as she looked across the room at the Duke of Eversley leading a Junoesque blond beauty onto the dance floor, it was as if the ballroom and everyone in it seemed to fade into the distance, leaving herself and the striking couple alone in the world.

Only gradually did she return to an awareness of her surroundings and Marian Horton still speculating on the identity of the beauty in Eversley's arms.

"She came with Sir Andrew Pettigrew and his wife. It may be that she is his widowed sister come to visit from town. I have heard it said that Eversley was used to be seen with her occasionally, but that was weeks ago. Doubtless she followed him here in the hope of taking up where they left off. And like the hero in a romance, he has discovered he really cannot live without her. Oh, isn't love wonderful, Miss Waincourt?"

Happily, Miranda, who inexplicably thought the duke in love with a blond Circe was anything but wonderful, was not given time to answer. For surprisingly she found herself surrounded by young men begging for a place on her dance card. As she was swept out onto the floor to take her place in a country set that was forming, she glimpsed Eversley lingering attentively at the edge of the dance floor next to the enticing Helen of Troy. Startled at the sudden way her fingers had inexplicably clenched into fists, Miranda forced herself to concentrate on the intricate patterns of the dance. Even so, she could not totally banish the disturbing riot of emotion that the view of the duke with another woman had aroused. Nor, as the evening wore inevitably on, was this the last time she saw them together. It soon became quite apparent to everyone present that the Duke of Eversley was paying marked attention to the voluptuous beauty.

The evening soon palled for Miranda, who attributed her sudden fit of the doldrums to a throbbing headache that had begun to plague her during the duke's first dance with his new inamorata. That and the fact that Pulvney seemed to have dropped off the edge of the earth, for she had seen nothing of the tall marquess all that evening, though Tess assured her he had, in the guise of Orion complete with club, sword, lion's skin and faithful dog Sirius, been in attendance earlier. Indeed, her cousin insisted, he had seemed most anxiously awaiting Miranda's arrival.

Even so, the supper dance inevitably arrived, and still without any sign of the delinquent marquess. Oh, botheration! Miranda inwardly fumed, for she found herself in the uncomfortable circumstance of being without an escort. Thinking to slip away unnoticed to her room, she turned to find Eversley before her, the sleepy blue eyes curiously intent upon her face.

"Oh!" She started, one hand rising convulsively to her suddenly heaving chest. "You startled me."

"I beg your pardon. That was not my intent."

"I wish you will not be idiotish," she snapped irritably. "I did not suppose that it was."

"You relieve my mind, Miss Waincourt," he rejoined with a gleam of amusement. "I had come to think you held me accountable for any and all of your misfortunes. But, indeed, I have come at your betrothed's insistence to claim the supper dance in his unavoidable absence. I fear Pulvney has become a trifle indisposed. It would seem that, like some women, even man's best friend cannot always be depended upon."

Miranda, able to make neither head nor tail of that cryptic remark, was nevertheless quite aware that Eversley had treated her to yet another of his reprehensible setdowns.

"I'm sure I cannot speak for man's best friend, my lord Duke," she retorted archly, "but I have found women to be of far greater reliability than the gamesters and ne'er-do-wells who appear to comprise the opposite gender. And though I am doubtless grateful to Pulvney for his belated thoughtfulness, I am feeling suddenly quite unreasonably tired. I believe I should prefer to wish you a good evening, my lord Duke, and retire."

"No doubt, my dear," said Eversley with a cold gleam of a smile that set Miranda's teeth on edge. "And yet I am not in the habit of being left standing by ill-mannered young ladies. Nor would your dubious reputation survive a second display of such unseemly behavior. You will cease instantly to make a spectacle of yourself and, smiling graciously, allow me to seat you and bring you a plate."

Miranda, who saw that they had indeed become the objects of unwelcome speculation, reluctantly allowed the duke to lead her to a seat at one of the long linen-covered tables set up for the midnight repast and waited on tenterhooks for him to fetch her a plate heaped almost indecently high with paper-thin ham, lobster patties, stuffed mushrooms and strawberries for which she had absolutely no appetite.

Uncomfortably aware that the duke's condescension had redeemed her in the eyes of her contemporaries, Miranda chafed at finding herself in the irritating nobleman's debt. Nor could she help but wonder why he should have put himself to the trouble when he so obviously held her beneath contempt. Greatly puzzled, she looked up to find the duke regarding her strangely.

"My lord Duke?" she questioned and to her chagrin felt a blush inexplicably color her cheeks.

"You know you really are the most exasperating female of my rather extensive acquaintance. Are you always so determined on self-destruction? Or is it only I who arouse this proclivity in you, Miss Waincourt? No, no. Do not fly up into the boughs, I beg you. Let us instead cry truce. I am charged by your betrothed to give you a message. Jeremy begs you will pardon him and asks that he be allowed to speak with you in private in the rose garden at the hour of ten tomorrow morning, if it is convenient."

"It is," she instantly affirmed, greatly relieved to have received a brief stay of execution in the matter of her unintentional betrothal and mystified by what she perceived as a leavening of the duke's mood. "Thank you," she added stiffly. "And now perhaps you shall see fit to relieve my curiosity. Where is Lord Pulvney? I have it on the most reliable of sources that he was here earlier, but he seems to have simply vanished."

"I am not at all certain, Miss Waincourt. But I should think he has found a quiet place in which to administer to his shattered nerves."

"You mean he is foxed?" she inquired in no little astonishment.

"He did not so appear when last I saw him," admitted the duke with an appreciative gleam of humor in the sleepy eyes. "But then, I had only the most fleeting glimpse, and it was dark at the time."

"I do wish you will stop bamming me, my lord," Miranda said, irritated and confused by the duke's sudden change of manner, for she found suddenly that she was able to recall only with difficulty that he was by far the most despicable man she had ever met and, further, that she was sure she quite thoroughly loathed him. "If Lord Pulvney is in some sort of difficulty, I would wish to know of it."

"No doubt, Miss Waincourt. It is only that I am very nearly certain Lord Pulvney would not thank me for divulging the circumstances of his—er—enforced retirement from Lady Tess's gala. However, if you insist..."

It soon transpired that Pulvney, unable to decide on a character suitable to his ungainly height, had been induced by his dearest friend Chums, the Earl of Chomney, to attend the ball as Orion, the giant hunter. Furthermore, the generous earl had taken it upon himself to negotiate from one Colonel Drake, formerly of the East India Company, the loan of the requisite lion's skin, sword and one prized hound to represent the ever-faithful Sirius. Orion's club he had left to Pulvney's invention. The earl, after arranging that the hound be brought to Pulvney at the ball itself in order that the marquess should not have the imposition of feeding and housing the animal until its presence was to be required, accepted his friend's heartfelt gratitude with aplomb and absented himself.

"However, it seems that Chums failed to inform poor Jeremy that the hound was used to accompany the colonel on his frequent forays into the wilds and was trained to a fierce dislike of anything remotely feline," Eversley remarked quite straight-faced. "No sooner had the animal scented the lion's skin that formed the greater part of our Orion's evening attire than it attacked. Tellingly, I might add. I fear Jeremy did not escape with a whole skin—though 'twas only the lion's that suffered—and was fortunate not to have incurred any injury...except, of course, to his nerves."

"B-but this is t-terrible!" Miranda stammered, hard put not to give way to mirth, for indeed she was all sympathy for the unfortunate Pulvney. Yet there was no denying the duke had related the tale with the masterful touch of one gifted with a keen sense of the absurd, a trait he held in common with Miranda.

Thus it was with eyes brimming over with shared laughter that their glances met and held. And suddenly neither was laughing anymore. Indeed, it seemed to Miranda that a shock passed through her entire frame from head to toe, to leave her oddly shaken. Nor could she tear her gaze from the eyes in which blue flames seemed somehow to have been ignited.

It was only with the greatest difficulty that she became aware at last that Chomney had come to claim her for his promised second dance.

Though she seemed stricken to the core by something she sensed but could not quite bring into definition, Miranda somehow found the presence of mind to rise and tender the duke an appropriate word of parting. Still, it was with a sense of unreality that she heard Chomney suggest they stroll for a time in the rose garden. Nodding absently, she permitted herself to be led from the ballroom through French doors into the blessed coolness of an evening breeze.

Vaguely she was aware that Chomney was speaking to her in great earnestness, and even managed an occasional monosyllabic utterance in response, but truth to tell, she heard not a single word that he said. Her thoughts were all on Eversley and the odd sensation that she had been struck by a thunderbolt. And suddenly everything became quite clear to her. She had fallen quite totally and irrevocably in love with the thoroughly detestable duke!

"Miss Waincourt—Miranda, my dear. I have never been one to wait patiently when anything so dear to my heart was involved. Nor can I tolerate the least rejection, and thus would rather forgo any lengthy speeches. I beg you will humor me and give me your answer now," Chomney ended. Then, when no answer at all seemed forthcoming, he felt compelled to add, "Miranda? Miss Waincourt."

"Wh-what?" faltered the lady, brought suddenly to a sense that Chomney was demanding a response of some sort to something he had said.

"I know this is unexpected and that you have had no time to prepare. A simple yes or no is all that I require."

Oh, botheration! Could the man not see she would just as lief be left alone? Vaguely she had heard him mention something about strolling hand in hand along a flower-strewn path and viewing together the panorama of life's simple pleasures, and though she very little anticipated being on hand in the near future for any sort of alfresco meanderings with the earl, she was in no state to dream up any plausible excuses.

"Oh, well, then," she said distractedly. "Yes, yes. I agree."

Whereupon she found herself suddenly crushed to a hard chest and held powerless in arms like steel bands.

"Miranda, my dear," Chomney breathed ardently against her hair. "You have made me the happiest of men."

"I—I have?" she queried in no little amazement.

"Like Pygmalion, I had little use for your sex and had thought never to be leg-shackled. But in you I have discovered my Galatea, my ideal of a perfect mate. You will never be sorry you have agreed to become my wife."

"Your wife?" Miranda gasped. "Is that what you asked of me? But I—I—"

"So, Miss Waincourt," came the cynical voice of doom at her back. "Or should I say Atalanta? For in the end it seems you have won the race. I offer you my congratulations for as brilliant and cold-blooded a campaign as it has been my privilege to witness. You have indeed conquered all three of the Inconquerables just as you intended from the very first."

Miranda, precipitously released by a startled Earl of Chomney, whirled with a stifled cry to behold the Duke of Eversley standing before her in his flowing chlamys and Ionic chiton like some vengeful Greek god.

"No. Oh, no, my lord. You don't understand," she began, raising one hand in eloquent supplication. But the duke's icy stare seemed to look right through her.

"You needn't put on your missish airs with me, Miss Waincourt," he jeered, sweeping her from head to toe with a contemptuous glance. "Or have you forgotten that I was the first to see through your façade of innocence? I know you for the heartless jade that you are."

Never had Miranda experienced such a raging fury as took her then. White-faced and trembling in every limb, she straightened to her full height to face her tormentor with blazing eyes.

"But then, there was little need to conceal my true nature from you, was there?" she said with a hard little laugh. "Once you had succumbed to my wiles. Indeed, I find I was disappointed that the greatest of the Inconquerables should have proved so easy a mark. I fear your reputation is greatly exaggerated, 'Evan darling.'"

For a moment Miranda, who could scarce believe in her own temerity, feared that she had gone too far as the livid-faced nobleman took a hasty step toward her. But then Chomney had stepped between them.

"Egad, Evan. Miranda. Have you both gone mad?"

The duke seemed only then to recall the earl's presence.

"No doubt," he said in an oddly heavy voice, "else I could never have believed I loved this Circe reincarnate. She's all yours, my friend. And may you never live to regret it as thoroughly as I have done.''

With that he turned and strode deliberately away, leaving Miranda to stare in impotent fury after him.

CHAPTER TWELVE

"YOU WILL DELIVER this note to the Earl of Chomney, Peggy. And inform John Coachman, if you please, that we shall be leaving immediately after nuncheon," Miranda said in a weary voice.

"Yes, miss." Peggy curtsied, her homely face expressive of pity for her employer. Miss Miranda looked worn to the nub, she did. And not from too much gaiety either, for unless she missed her guess, those were tears that had dampened her mistress's pillow.

"Oh, and, Peggy," Miranda added with unwonted sternness as the abigail turned to go, "Be sure to come back as soon as you can, to help finish with the packing. I want *nothing* to delay our departure for Groves."

"Yes, Miss Miranda," said the girl dutifully and, thinking that her mistress was of certain in a rare taking, fled from the room.

Alone at last, Miranda heaved a sigh and sank wearily onto the bed, her forehead pressed against one hand resting on the bedpost. She had not slept a wink the night before, but had relived over and over the dreadful scene with Eversley and the discovery that she had been so foolish as to fall in love with a man who believed her a doxy and a scheming jade. It really was too lowering, she thought with a flash of revivifying indignation. But that quickly faded before an even greater heaviness of spirit, leaving her unwontedly listless. So this was what it was to be in love, she mused wryly and felt a pang of remorse for the two Inconquerables who had professed an undying affection for her, going so far as to ask her hand in marriage. And now she faced the unpleasant duty of attempting to explain how she came to be engaged to them both at the same time and, furthermore, why she could marry neither of them.

It was with a horrid sense of unreality that she, who had always considered herself a wholly sensible female, found herself embroiled in so utterly absurd a predicament. She should have thought that at least Chomney, after Eversley's diatribe against her, would have immediately cried off, but, raving something about His Grace being up to his old tricks again and having contrived the whole out of pique at having lost the game, he had not seemed to place any credence in the duke's outrageous accusations. Indeed, he had been indignant and no little put out with his friend, even going so far as to declare his intention of calling Eversley out to clear his lady's name. Miranda blushed in mortification, recalling the stratagem to which she had at last been forced in order to distract the raving nobleman from so blatant an absurdity. To think that she, Miranda Waincourt, a follower of Mrs. Wollstonecraft, should have sunk so low as to affect a swoon! It went beyond the bounds of decency. Never again would she be able to hold her head up. And in the end it had only prolonged the inevitable, for she had still to tell the earl that she could never marry him. Thus the necessity of the note asking him to meet her at ten o'clock in the rose garden, the appointed time and place of her assignation with Pulvney. She would see them together and have the business done with once and for all.

Oh, why had she not remained at Groves where she belonged? She sighed. None of the foibles perpetrated by her enterprising siblings could possibly compare with what *she* had accomplished in just two weeks at Applegarth. Nor could any of the multitude of problems awaiting her at home loom so hopelessly as those which she had incurred on her first excursion into society.

No sooner had that thought taken form than an imperious knock sounded at her door.

"Miranda! Come out at once. Allie has run away with that blasted billy goat."

"ALL OF THIS absurd imbroglio is your fault, Miranda," observed the young sprig dressed to the nines in a Jean de Bry coat, the sleeves of which were voluminously padded at the shoulder seams to an absurd height totally in keeping with the heavily starched shirt points that threatened at any moment to pierce his ears. "If you had done your duty and married Sir Percival, none of this would have happened. Allie would have had a sensible governess who would never have allowed her to form a tendre for a billy goat with the poor taste to raid old Mistress Graves's herb garden. And, furthermore, you would not now be on the shelf and perilously close to your last prayers. Our father was much too lenient with you.''

''Enough, Harry!'' Miranda snapped in anger and bitter remorse as she turned to face her eldest brother. Was it not bad enough that poor little Allie had been missing for nearly sixteen hours and that Sir Percival had no doubt frightened her half to death upon coming to Groves, an ancient blunderbuss in hand, with the intention of putting her beloved Hannibal away? It was, of course, reprehensible that Bertie had bitten the old reprobate on the calf and that Kit had seen fit to topple him into the ornamental lake while Allie had fled into the home woods with Hannibal safely in tow. Yet she simply could not find it in her heart to blame any of them. Indeed, she was proud of the way they had stood together in defense of home and family.

''This is taking us nowhere,'' she said, striving to be calm. ''I know I should never have abandoned the children to Aunt Agatha's sole care. The poor dear. What she must be suffering! But what's done is done. It now remains for us to find Allie and somehow persuade Sir Percival not to put a period to Hannibal's existence. Allie's health and happiness depend on it.''

''Well, as to that,'' interjected the youth with a condescension that would have set his sister on her guard had she not been fairly distracted with worry for her little sister, ''Sir Percy indicated to me that he would not be averse to forgetting the whole matter upon condition that you reconsider his offer of marriage. Naturally, I assured him that you would allow him to pay his addresses as soon as ever Allie can be safely returned to the bosom of her family.''

"You did *what*?" Miranda uttered in awful tones, scarce able to believe her ears. "How dared you, Henry Waincourt! By what right should you have told him any such tissue of lies?"

"Well, I am head of the family," he pointed out, eyeing Miranda's white-lipped fury in sudden wariness. "And besides, it appeared the only way out of this coil, which, I might add, was of your making. I fail to see what else I might have done."

"No doubt," she agreed coldly. Then, knowing from past experience the futility of attempting to bring the latest Earl of Waring to any real sense of responsibility, she dismissed him from her mind. She would keep her appointment with the two noblemen. She owed them that. But then she must make her way to Groves with as much dispatch as was humanly possible. And the devil fly away with Henry Waincourt.

Feverishly she laid her plans. It had taken her nearly twelve hours to reach Applegarth in the old Waincourt travel carriage. But if she were to go cross-country on Aster, she could easily cut the time in half. Peggy could follow with her belongings in the carriage. She would have need only of a pair of her brother's riding breeches, an old work coat she had stuck in purely out of habit and her boots. But first the breeches, she thought, turning to fix her brother with narrowed eyes.

"WE OUGHT NOT to have let her go like that, Chums," Pulvney said, shaking his head in the manner of one who has cogitated deeply on a ponderous subject only to discover his earlier conclusions had been wrong.

"Don't see that we could have done any different, old chap," replied the Earl of Chomney with a seriousness totally foreign to his usual insouciance. "Not after that young jackanapes—damme, did you ever see such a coat!—who claimed t'be her legal guardian, made it clear he considered it was none of our business. Besides, Miss Waincourt turned us both down. Mind you, I still think the world of the chit and I daresay she was right when she said we shouldn't suit. After all—" and he gave a slight shudder "—I can't exactly see either you or I taking on another man's family. And though Miranda would almost make it worth the sacrifice, since I doubt there could ever be a dull moment with her as one's wife, still I ain't one to handle rejection at all well. You know that, Jer. No doubt when all is said and done, we are well out of it."

The Marquess of Pulvney eyed his friend thoughtfully for a long moment. He was not at all sure he agreed with Chomney on that last, though he, too, had begun to have some reservations about his proposed nuptials after the earl had searched him out the night before to relate the bizarre tale of the normally imperturbable duke and the fiery-tempered redhead. But not so much because his sentiments had been altered, for indeed they had not been, but because it had suddenly occurred to him that Miranda's best interests might not be served by marrying him. He liked her far too well to saddle her with a slow top like himself when it seemed quite likely she had formed a tendre for someone much better suited to her quick wit and high spirit.

"But still," he said at last, in his ponderous manner, "someone ought to follow to make sure she reaches home all in one piece. It's a cinch the Earl of Waring can't be depended on to be of any help. And well, if things shouldn't work out with the little girl and all, she'll need somebody to help her over the rough spots."

The Earl of Chomney paused in his own mental perambulations to scrutinize his companion with a jaundiced eye.

"All right, Jeremy. Out with it," he interjected with none of the usual amused tolerance reserved for Pulvney's roundaboutations. "*Whom* did you have in mind?"

"Chums, does it occur to you that our Miranda might not be so indifferent to Evan as she claims t'be? I mean, don't it strike you as a trifle odd that she should make us both promise to keep mum about all this where Eversley was concerned?"

"Now that you mention it, Jeremy," Chomney rejoined with suddenly arrested interest, "it was *deuced* odd. The chit could hardly even say his name. Just sort of choked it out. And wouldn't look at either one of us. Of ocurse," he mused, tugging thoughtfully at his chin, "it could be that the lady was still in high dudgeon. I've never seen anyone quite so infuriated. Or quite so gloriously beautiful," he added with a tinge of regret. "And who can blame her? Evan called her some pretty hard names. Come to think of it, I've never seen Evan so incensed. It ain't like him to dub a lady a trollop and a doxy, not even if she is one—

which Miss Waincourt certainly is not. Bad ton, y'know. And not at all in Evan's style."

"That's it, then, isn't it?" pronounced the marquess with an air of finality. "It's plain as the nose on your face, Chester. Miranda Waincourt has fallen head over ears in love with Eversley. And unless I miss my guess, Evan is in the same case. Now, what are we going to do about it?"

Thus it was that Evan Westlake, Duke of Eversley, was rousted from his bed before noon by two of his closest intimates. The unheralded event, however, did little to endear them to His Grace, who, after storming out of the rose garden in a cold rage the night before, had attempted to vent his spleen on four full decanters of port. With a telling groan, the duke opened bleary eyes and greeted his two morning callers with something less than his usual urbanity.

"This had better be a matter of life and death," he growled in no uncertain terms, "else you shall find yourselves most definitely in the lurch."

"Easy, old man," soothed Chomney. "No need to fly up into the boughs."

"That's right, Evan. We just dropped in to say goodbye," Pulvney offered. "And to tell you no hard feelings. The best man won."

"I was not aware we were involved in a competition. Or are you referring to the scheming little demirep who managed to take us all in?"

"Now hold on, Evan," Chomney interjected frostily. "You've no call to besmirch the lady's name. Damme if she ain't too good for you. But by some bizarre twist of fate, she fell for you. What we want to know is, what are your intentions?''

''I beg your pardon,'' drawled the duke ominously. ''I had thought my intentions made quite clear. After all,'' he added with a cold glimmer of a smile, ''the 'lady' has betrothed herself to you and Pulvney. Henceforth, I intend to have nothing to do with the little doxy.''

''Either Chums or I should like nothing better than to stand Miss Waincourt's friend in need,'' Pulvney said, his thoughtful gaze on the duke's stony aspect. ''However, she has tied our hands by refusing us both.''

''How not, when such was her plan all along?'' the duke observed with a cold glitter of his blue eyes.

''As to that,'' mused the marquess, ''we cannot agree. It was you, after all, who maneuvered her into the uncomfortable position of appearing to have accepted my proposal. The lady herself never gave me any indication that she regarded me as other than a friend. Nor did she once favor me with an affirmative answer. Indeed, I was well aware she intended to reject my proposal, and put her off in the hope that time would be my ally.''

''And I suppose she did not jilt Chomney either,'' the duke drawled, raising an arrogant eyebrow in disbelief.

''Exactly so,'' admitted that worthy with an odd twist of the lips. ''I thought at the time Miss Waincurt was uncommonly distracted. Demmed peculiar, if you ask me. Fifteen minutes with you and she's all atwitter. Never even heard me pour my heart out to her. Just gave me the first answer that came to her mind without even knowing she was pledging to become my wife. Damme, Evan, some men have all the luck.''

"I'd say we are all fortunate to have escaped the lady's coils," the duke sneered, but with a peculiar glint in his eyes. "And now if you will kindly remove yourselves, I find I am become uncommonly weary of the entire subject."

Whereupon a sharp rap on His Grace's bedroom door followed by Sir Charles Davenforth's harried entrance took them all by surprise.

"Evan, you've got to do something. It was bad enough waking up to find that popinjay Waring on our doorstep—and what must he do but send Miranda riding *ventre à terre* across country on some wild-goose chase—but now there's the devil to pay with Tess. She knows, Evan, all about the blasted wager."

"Wager? What wager?" queried a mystified Marquess of Pulvney.

A heartfelt sigh was heard to emanate from the much beleaguered duke at the sudden popularity of his private quarters.

"Very well, Charles," he murmured resignedly and, flinging aside the bedclothes, rose to don a magnificent example of the Déshabille, which set off his broad-shouldered, narrow-waisted frame to the envy of his three friends. "I perceive that Miss Waincourt has landed herself in some new coil from which it devolves somehow upon me to deliver her."

"Indeed, Evan," remarked a highly incensed feminine voice from the doorway, "for though you have the reputation of a rake, I had not thought you so devoid of feeling as to ruin an innocent female's name. To think that if Charles had not the fortunate propensity for talking in his sleep, I might never have known about this thoroughly reprehensible wager!"

"The fruits of a troubled conscience, no doubt," Pulvney observed darkly.

"And now what will become of her I shudder to think," Tess continued as though she had not been rudely interrupted. "Even if she does not come to grief ere she reaches Groves, her brother has promised her hand in marriage to a reputed roué more than twice her age and possessed of a half-grown brood of miscreants. Oh, Evan! I shall never forgive you!"

"Now, Tess," expostulated her scandalized spouse, in a vain attempt to draw her from the room, "need I remind you a gentleman's boudoir is no place for a lady?"

"Oh, really, Charles," offered the Earl of Chomney, settling himself comfortably in a wing chair the better to enjoy what promised to be an uncommonly stimulating morning call. "Surely we need not rest on formality where the goddess of love is concerned. Who is more deserving than she to see the farce through?"

"You need remind me of nothing, Charles," Tess retorted, pointedly ignoring the earl's unfortunate tendency toward levity. "Indeed, you have already recalled to mind my mother's warning of your unstable character. For you must know, Charles, she was never convinced that we should suit, and now I cannot wonder but that she was right. To think you should have made my cousin the object of a wager. How *could* you have been so insensitive to my feelings, let alone Miranda's?''

"Indeed, how could you, Charles?'' expostulated the earl, apparently much struck at his friend's hitherto unsuspected iniquitous nature.

"What wager, Charles?'' queried Pulvney in deadly calm, his protracted drawl markedly in abeyance. "If you and Evan have in any way dishonored the lady, you shall both have me to answer to.''

But the duke, who had stiffened to attention at Tess's initial speech, apparently had no intention of listening to a disputation on Sir Charles's alleged vagaries of character, or his own for that matter.

"Silence! All of you!'' he thundered, upon which all discussion magically ceased.

"Now, my dearest Tess,'' he drawled in such a manner as to leave no doubt in that lady's mind that the sleepy pussycat was at last and irrevocably quite fully aroused. "You will be pleased to explain this farrago of nonsense concerning your cousin's latest debacle. While I cannot doubt that the appallingly intrepid Miss Waincourt might be witless enough to take off cross-country without benefit of escort or chaperone, I find it fantastic that even so devious a conniver as our sworn spinster should find herself already embarked upon a *third* betrothal of marriage. I warn you, Tess, this smacks of one of your matchmaking ploys, of which, I might add, I am heartily tired.''

"To think I have lived to hear you insult me, Evan Westlake,'' said a much distraught Lady Tess, sniffing. "And after all the trouble to which I have gone on your behalf! Luring Miranda from her beloved Groves. Seeing to it that she never once suspected she was the means by which I meant to teach the Inconquerables a much needed lesson of the heart. And indeed, you cannot deny that she touched each of you, even as I knew she would. For she is truly an innocent and deserving of much better than any of you. But to think my well-intentioned manipulations should have brought about her ruination—which will be the case if she is indeed forced to marry Sir Percival Peregrine—I hold myself responsible. And if anything has happened to Allie, Miranda will undoubtedly hold herself to blame. Nor shall I ever be able to forgive myself."

"Allie! What has Miss Waincourt's infant sister to do with anything?" inquired a still-wary duke, his heart, nonetheless, beginning to pound with sudden, unmistakable alarm. In response, Tess was induced to relate in its entirety the tale of the Waincourt runaway.

"You must believe this is not a ploy, Evan," she finished, dabbing at her eyes with a wisp of lace. "Indeed, I heartily wish never to play the matchmaker again if only you will go after Miranda and see that no harm comes to her."

"If all you say is true, then I should like to meet this remarkably irresponsible Earl of Waring," the duke said, an exceedingly dangerous glitter in his deceptively heavy-lidded eyes.

His wish was immediately to be gratified.

"I say," interposed a new arrival in the duke's already crowded boudoir, "could one of you kindly direct me to the breakfast room? I've had nothing since a remarkably unprepossessing inn some dozen or so miles from here and find myself devilish sharp set."

"Ah, the Earl of Waring, I must presume," Eversley observed, taking in without a bat of an eyelash the young exquisite's sartorial splendor. "I beg you will come in, my lord. It would seem that you and I have a matter of some importance to discuss. If, that is, we may be granted a measure of privacy?" he added, pointedly arching an imperious eyebrow at his host of uninvited morning callers.

THE PROPOSED INTERVIEW between duke and earl lasted no longer than it took for His Grace of Eversley to enlighten the young coxcomb on the efficacies of a Corinthian's exceedingly handy pair of fives. After that, the duke helped the bewildered young man to his feet, dusted him off, and informed him in no uncertain terms that not only would Miss Waincourt never wed Sir Percival Peregrine, but the future Duchess of Eversley would expect him to take especial care that nothing untoward befell either Allie Waincourt or the admittedly reprehensible Hannibal till they should be safely removed to Eversley, along with the delightful Aunt Agatha and two scrubby schoolboys.

Thus it was that some six hours later, Bertram Waincourt, stealing surreptitiously across the home meadow immediately to the south of Groves, came suddenly upon an elegantly attired gentleman reclining at his ease, his back propped against one of the many towering oaks from which the estate took its name.

"Ah," remarked the gentleman, eyeing the boy from his unkempt thatch of fiery hair to the scuffed toes of his well-worn shoes, "I observe a certain family resemblance to your elder sister totally lacking in your scapegrace eldest brother. You possess her chin, expressive, I've not a doubt, of the same damnably stubborn nature, and her eyes and mouth, both indicative of a reprehensible levity. I have, I believe, the honor of addressing Bertram Waincourt, have I not?"

Young Waincourt, having instantly recognized the Duke of Eversley from his sister's description, perceived as well from the gleam of tolerant amusement in the exceedingly sleepy blue eyes that His Grace was top-of-the-trees and a right 'un.

"You've got me pegged, Your Grace," he answered with boyish frankness and grinned as the duke's aristocratic eyebrow quizzically arched. "Oh, I guessed who you were, right enough. Sassy wrote us all about you and your two friends. Did you ride all this way just to see Miranda?"

"All in good time," the duke drawled unconcernedly. "Actually, it's you I'm interested in at present. I saw you coming through the wood and decided to await your arrival."

"And what'd you want me for, I wonder?" queried the boy with an impish grin strongly reminiscent of his elder sister's. "It seemed to me Sassy had taken you in dislike, m'lord. It might be she won't welcome you at Groves."

"Quite possibly, bantling," the duke agreed with the glimmer of a smile. "And you, I suspect, might pave the way for me."

Bertie shrugged fatalistically.

"I might, though I ain't making any promises I can get you in. You can never tell with Miranda. Is that your horse?" he exclaimed, spying the gray stallion grazing a few feet away. "I say, he's a prime bit o' blood. Just wait'll Kit sees him. No wonder Cousin Charles put up his bay against him. I expect I'd've done the same."

"It would appear Miss Waincourt has left nothing out of the telling," the duke observed dryly. "May I thus assume that she has arrived home safely?"

"You weren't worried about Sassy, were you?" the boy asked, leaving no doubt in the duke's mind that he had slipped a notch or two in the boy's estimation. "She beat you by a couple of hours anyway."

"Considering she had nearly a three hours' start on me, I am not displeased with Agincourt's performance," rejoined His Grace complacently. "However, I did not put myself to the trouble of riding neck or nothing all the way from Kent to ascertain which was the faster mount. It was brought to my attention that Miss Waincourt has been called away from her cousin's through a certain misunderstanding over the reprehensible Hannibal. Perhaps you could enlighten me on the status of your sister's most recent coil. Have Hannibal and the devoted Allie been safely returned?"

Bertram Waincourt lifted guileless green eyes to the nobleman's face.

"Like as not Allie's been carried off by Gypsies by now, Your Grace," he confided with a mournful air.

"Unfortunate, to say the least," drawled the duke, apparently unmoved by such an eventuality. "Upon what evidence do you base your theory?"

"Well, half the neighborhood has been out scouring the countryside day and night since she and Hannibal ran off. And nobody's found anything yet. Sir Percy wanted to drag the lake, but Miranda wouldn't hear of it. You should've heard her put old spindle-shanks in his place," he said, his freckled face expressive of rapture tinged with awe.

"A rare privilege, no doubt," granted Eversley, no stranger to Miss Waincourt in a high dudgeon.

"She was awful mad. Said it was all his fault if anything bad had happened to Allie and that he should've known better'n to threaten children and defenseless old ladies with guns. Then she told him to get off Waincourt land and never show his face there again. But that was nothing compared to what came next."

"There's more? And better? You astound me," drawled the duke, apparently fascinated by the promised treat.

"Well, Sir Percy went all sort of white and told her she'd sing a different tune when Harry got back. You see, Harry's the head of the family and he'd promised Sir Percy Sassy'd marry him to make things right."

"Ah. The third betrothal. All begins to become clear to me."

"I beg your pardon, sir?" queried the boy at the duke's seeming irrelevance.

"Never mind, bantling. You were saying?"

"Well, Miranda told him pigs'd fly before she ever married the likes of him. Then Sir Percy got ugly. Said it was all over the county how she was playing it fast and loose at her toplofty cousin's with some high-flying lords that belonged to the Carlton Set. But even so, he said, he was willing to give her the protection of his name, and when she was his wife, he'd teach her the humility proper to a female. Then he grabbed her and tried to kiss her. And that's when Miranda let him have it. Landed him a facer as neat as Gentleman Jim himself could've done."

"Good Lord! A pugilist as well as an advocate of women's rights! What other secret delights does the inimitable Miss Waincourt have in store for me, I wonder. Tell me, is there a history of madness in your family, or is your elder sister the only candidate for Bedlam?"

"You're bamming me, ain't you, Your Grace? I know a complete hand when I see one."

"I'm quite sure you do, halfling. As do I. Now, don't you think it's time you told me where to find Allie?"

CHAPTER THIRTEEN

"YOU MUST NOT blame yourself, Aunt," Miranda said, solicitously hugging the elderly woman about the shoulders. "You did the best you could under the circumstances, though I do wish you might have let me know about everything sooner."

"No, you have every right to be angry with me," sniffed a greatly distraught Aunt Agatha, who proceeded nervously to shred her lace handkerchief. "I've made a terrible mull of everything. But indeed I never thought things would go so far. I meant only to hold the old lady off till you should have had your chance to experience a little of what you have been denied through no fault of your own. And now what has come of it? Your reputation is in ruins. Doubtless the tale of your quarrel with Sir Percival is already common knowledge throughout the country. Perhaps it would be best if Allie remains in hiding forever, for I expect at any time the magistrate will come to send us all to Newgate."

"Nonsense!" Miranda sternly admonished and wondered uneasily if the poor dear were coming unhinged from worry over Allie, for she was finding it nigh impossible to make any sense of her aunt's disjointed utterances. "I promise you Allie will be found, unharmed and bubbling over about her grand adventure.''

''Oh, no doubt,'' Aunt Agatha agreed with the air of a doomsday prophet. ''And then where shall we be? Who would have thought Sir Percy would rouse half the county to search for Allie? The bothersome old fool. And when everything in the end comes to light, we shall be a laughingstock. Oh, the scandal! Why must I be a meddlesome old woman with more hair than wit? And yet it seemed at the time such a simple matter. I simply cannot understand where things went wrong.''

Miranda, who had already spent a fruitless two hours searching out every place she could think of in which a little girl and a ravenous goat might conceivably hide themselves, was as close to exhaustion and utter hopelessness as she had ever been in her life. Nor was she in any state to deal at all rationally with her kinswoman's apparent vagaries, not with Allie still not found and dusk of her second night away from home fast approaching. Indeed, it was all Miranda could do to keep from screaming in utter frustration. Thus she could perhaps be excused for mistaking her aunt's confused ramblings as the natural manifestations of guilt and anxiety for the missing Allie.

''You must not despair, dearest Aunt,'' she said bracingly. ''You know how I depend on you to keep everything running smoothly here while I am gone in search of Allie. Now, promise me you will lie down for an hour or two. Indeed, I warn you that I shall send Miss Melbourne up to see that you do.''

"I'm afraid that is not at all possible, my dear," Aunt Agatha said distractedly. "You may try, of course, but you will only discover that Miss Melbourne is nowhere to be found. For you must know she is a wholly sensible governess and would not dream of allowing one of her charges to wander about the countryside unprotected."

Miranda regarded the figure of her aunt, rather unwontedly subdued in lavender brocade with a wig swept high from the forehead *à la Pompadour* and dyed to match her dress, in no little astonishment.

"What are you saying, Aunt?" she queried with sudden keen interest. "Did Miss Melbourne have some notion where Allie might be hiding? Has she gone off to look on her own?"

"Oh, dear," muttered the eccentric spinster, appearing suddenly to grow quite flustered, "I suppose one could say that."

"But, Aunt Agatha, why didn't you tell me before? Surely Miss Melbourne gave some hint as to where she was going. How long has she been gone?"

"As to that, I couldn't say exactly," Aunt Agatha responded, waving her handkerchief vaguely in the air. "Indeed, I cannot seem to recall having seen her recently. Which is not at all remarkable when one considers the strain I have been under. I am not, after all, as young as I was used to be, Miranda. Indeed, I shouldn't wonder if I am not about to become extremely unwell."

It was only by virtue of the greatest self-control that Miranda did not herself succumb to a fit of the vapors. For it soon became quite obvious that she was going to learn nothing more from her aunt, who did, indeeed, display every sign of one hovering on the brink of a sharp decline.

"Surely none of this is to the point, Miranda," uttered the elderly lady in the piteous accents of one unjustly subjected to the Spanish Inquisition. In a gesture of weary distraction, she touched the fingers of either hand to her temples and sank weakly on to a dimity-covered sofa. "No doubt Miss Melbourne will find her way home when she's of a mind to," she added, draping her rapidly wilting form across the single roll-over arm of the sofa. "Though by then we shall no doubt be on our way to the penal colonies. Then who shall see to Allie? The poor dear will likely grow up in the woods like one of those wild children reared by wolves or bears or what have you. And however will she make a suitable match, for what man would have her? You must know I would tell you where she has gone if only I could remember."

Miranda, greatly alarmed at her aunt's wild ravings, experienced an instant pang of remorse. Poor Aunt Agatha. No doubt in Miranda's own overwrought state she had taxed the aging spinster rather too severely.

"Of course you would," she said contritely. "I'm afraid I have been thinking only of myself, when you have had to carry all the burden far longer than you should have done. But I'm here now. And you will feel more the thing after a little nap."

"Perhaps you are right, my dear," sighed the elderly lady, meekly allowing Miranda to lead her to her bed. "I'm sure I shall be of better use remaining out of everyone's way. If only you had someone other than a bumbling old woman with whom to share your troubles, Miranda,'' she added woefully. ''I had such high hopes that... Well, it little matters now. I have quite managed to ruin everything for you.''

"Oh, Aunt,'' Miranda chided tenderly. ''You must not think such things. You know none of us could get along without you. You rest now. And please don't worry. I know Allie is fine.''

"She has to be,'' Miranda added to herself as she softly closed the door on Aunt Agatha dozing fitfully on her bed. But nevertheless she shuddered, recalling Sir Percival's odious assurance that her young sister had doubtless in her hasty flight fallen into the far side of the lake bordered by the dense spinney of oaks. Sternly she took herself in hand. Allie, she told herself quite firmly, was holed up in one of the numerous hiding places she and Bertie had discovered on their daily forays into the woods. Indeed, if ever she laid her hands on her youngest brother, Miranda suspected that he could be made to reveal a great deal concerning Allie's whereabouts, for had she not seen him stealing away shortly after her disastrous confrontation with Sir Percival, and had he not been carrying a suspicious-looking bundle that he had sought to conceal from her? Oh, she would string him up by the thumbs if he had helped Allie to remain in hiding! Things had gone too far, indeed, if the boy could be so heartless as to allow poor Aunt Agatha to suffer such anguish.

Wearily she shoved such thoughts aside as she made her way downstairs to the book room with the vague notion of seeking out a place where she might think undisturbed. There must be some place that had not yet occurred to her which Allie or the boys might have mentioned at one time or another.

The rambling old house, which she had always considered quite warm and homey, seemed unbearably empty with Kit and most of the servants gone in search of Allie, and with Bertie the Lord only knew where. Perhaps the Oriental rug on the floor in the library did appear a bit worn after the quiet elegance of Applegarth, she thought, noticing for the first time an almost insignificant rent in the woven fabric. And perhaps the matching caffoy-covered wing chairs and settee were a trifle faded, but in the muted light of the late-afternoon sun slanting through the open French windows, the room still retained a quiet beauty of its own.

Applegarth! It already seemed as if an eternity had passed since she had looked into laughing blue eyes and known she would never after be as she was before. Indeed, except for an aching hollowness within, Applegarth and all that had happened there might be naught but a disturbing dream or a tale told to her about some other luckless female witless enough to fall victim to the Duke of Eversley's fatal charm. How could she have been so idiotish as to believe that she should somehow be immune? Had she not been forewarned by Cousin Tess that the duke was a notorious rake infamous for the long line of hapless victims left behind him? Oh, how she detested him, she told herself, and then immediately recalled an image of Eversley entertaining her in the library at Applegarth with a keen wit and an ease of manner that she had not found at all distasteful. And, too, Eversley bending over her in unaffected concern as she lay stunned after the fall from Aster. Indeed, she seemed plagued by a kaleidescope of Eversleys, all of whom in one way or another fitted her notion of the ideal man.

Oh, botheration! she thought in sudden anger. She was tired indeed if she could sit around mooning over a man who had done nothing but insult her from the moment they had met. In truth, the duke was utterly contemptible, and doubtless what she thought was love was actually nothing more than a momentary affliction, like the measles or the mumps, to which everyone must succumb at one time or another but which soon would pass once it had run its natural course. After all, she was hardly the romantic type who was likely to fall into a decline because of an unrequited love, she told herself quite firmly. Indeed, she had no intention of giving the Duke of Eversley any such satisfaction as he no doubt would have enjoyed at anything so patently absurd.

Satisfied that she had at last relegated the matter to its proper perspective, Miranda dragged her weary body from the wing chair fronting the former earl's oversized oakwood desk and, turning, locked glances with those very same infuriatingly sleepy blue eyes which had never ceased to haunt her.

"*You!*" she gasped, raking with her astonished gaze the long, lean form elegantly attired in buckskin unmentionables and a bottle-green riding jacket that could have been cut only by Weston. "How did you get into my house?"

Slowly the duke straightened to favor her with a mocking bow.

"I shall not answer the obvious, Miss Waincourt," he drawled with the cynical twist of the lips that had never failed to set Miranda on fighting edge. "Suffice it to say that I should have had myself announced had there been anyone to receive me. But, alas! Reliable help is difficult to come by, is it not? Especially in the country."

"Oh," she said, coloring slightly as she realized Dunton, the Waincourts' aging butler, must be out with the others still searching for Allie. But how typical of the insufferable duke to catch her on the wrong foot. Her small pointed chin rose in unconscious pride. "Actually we do not lack for competent retainers, Your Grace. As it happens, you have chosen an unpropitious time to call on us uninvited."

"Oh, but I should never be so remiss, Miss Waincourt," demurred the duke infuriatingly. "Actually, the Earl of Waring was most anxious to assure me that I should be quite welcome in his home, even going so far as to allow that I should be considered a part of the family, as it were, and as such might run tame about the place."

"I was not aware, Your Grace, that you were acquainted with my eldest brother," Miranda rejoined, eyeing the duke with obvious suspicion.

"No, how could you? I was granted that rather dubious pleasure only this morning," commented the duke reminiscently. "But we parted on the most amicable of terms, I assure you."

Miranda, who could not possibly conceive of any circumstances under which the arrogant duke and her scapegrace eldest brother could be on terms, amicable or otherwise, found herself at *point non plus*, for no matter how she might wish to do so, she could not call a premier nobleman of the realm an out-and-out liar.

Thus, deeming a strategic retreat the better part of valor, she assumed a demure manner totally at variance with the glint of her emerald eyes.

"Be that as it may, Your Grace," she said in dulcet tones. "At present everyone in the household is otherwise occupied. And I myself was on the point of leaving. Consequently, I'm afraid I cannot offer you the hospitality due a peer of the realm."

"And what sort would that be, Miss Waincourt? For *this* peer of the realm, *if* you were not called upon to leave so precipitously? Finger screws and hot tar, perhaps?" he mused sardonically and, to her discomfiture, strolled languidly across the room to stand looking down at her from his not inconsiderable height. "And no doubt I should deserve them."

"No doubt," she retorted acidly, meeting his glance with a withering blaze of exotically slanted eyes, upon which she discovered that the duke was not quite so elegant as she had at first supposed. Indeed, she espied a small square of court plaster affixed to one side of the lean jaw as if His Grace had cut himself shaving. Furthermore, his raven locks, usually painstakingly brushed to appear fashionably disheveled, seemed rather more tousled than was strictly acceptable even for the windswept look. Yet more telling than either of the aforementioned defects were the normally sleepy blue eyes, which upon closer inspection were unmistakably bloodshot.

"However, despite the fact that I may be a trollop and a manipulator of poor, unsuspecting men," she continued with cool disdain, "the Waincourts as a rule do not resort to torturing invited guests—even those who are unutterably contemptible."

"Oh, bravo, Miss Waincourt," applauded the duke. "I see your wit has not lost its cutting edge. I am no doubt relieved to find you the same little spitfire that first endeared herself to me. Indeed, I have since discovered that not only are you able to cut a man down to size with the sharpness of your tongue, but if all else fails, you may just as easily fell him with a handy pair of fives."

"Oh!" Miranda exclaimed on an explosive breath and to her chagrin felt the blood rush ignominiously to her cheeks. "It would seem you have been uncommonly busy since arriving, my lord Duke. From what tattlemonger have you garnered that charming *on dit*?"

"I suspect so scintillating a tale must by now be common knowledge in the county, Miss Waincourt. No doubt you are in the way of fast becoming something of a local legend. How many women, after all, have had the dubious honor not only of landing the local magistrate a facer, but of rejecting as well four proposals of marriage in a single fortnight? I cannot but speculate," he ended with an oddly ironic twist of the lips, "who will be your next unwitting victim."

Miranda, who was fast developing a throbbing headache, found herself sorely tempted to add murder to her growing infamies.

"I can assure you there is no end to the list of likely candidates," she said in bitter sarcasm. "Miss Charity Graves herself has informed me that her dear brother, our own beloved rector, is not at all indifferent to me and could do worse than marry a poor spinster who finds herself nearly upon the shelf. And of course, one cannot yet rule out Sir Percival, who thus far has demonstrated a tenacity of purpose that must certainly delight even the coldest-hearted femme fatale. Naturally I could go on and on, but I see little point in boring you with a complete catalog of all the eligible bachelors within my unsavory sphere of influence. Indeed, it is no doubt with the greatest of reluctance that I feel compelled to bring this less than edifying interview to an end. I *was* about to depart on a matter of some urgency."

"Ah, yes, the missing Allie," interpolated the duke, taking from his pocket an exquisite Sèvres snuffbox and flicking open the lid with his thumb. "I wondered when we should come at last to the purpose of my visit. Tell me, as a matter of idle curiosity, is it your usual practice to abandon at the slightest provocation all caution and in masculine attire to ride cross-country without benefit of a male escort? Not, of course, that you do not present a rather prepossessing figure in a gentleman's unmentionables," he added, eyeing her slender, breeches-clad form with sardonic appreciation, "but it would seem behavior better suited to a complete hoyden."

"What I do is hardly any of your affair, my lord Duke," Miranda retorted, made blushingly aware of her altogether disreputable appearance. "Nor can I possibly imagine what Allie should have to do with your following me to Groves. Just why have you come?"

To Miranda's rapidly mounting irritation, Eversley, drawing forth between thumb and forefinger a pinch of his favorite mixture, inhaled, closed and replaced the snuffbox in his coat pocket, then brushed an imaginary fleck from his sleeve before deigning to answer.

"I should have thought it quite obvious, Miss Waincourt," he said without a flicker of an eyelid. "I have come at your cousin's behest to relieve you of your anxiety concerning the wretched child and the totally infamous Hannibal."

"I beg your pardon?" queried Miranda, incredulous at the cool effrontery of the man. "I'm sure you will forgive me if I find it rather difficult to believe that anyone so noted for his indolent nature should put himself to so much trouble—and for a female he holds beneath contempt. No, my lord. That is doing it much too brown. Indeed, I feel compelled to question your ulterior motives."

"Do not think," returned the duke balefully, "that I have not repeatedly questioned my own rationality since being rudely roused from my bed this morning at a wholly unprecedented hour. I believe I have ever entertained a certain tolerance for the foibles of my fellowmen, Miss Waincourt, but I can say without reservation that I find being harangued by three of my closest intimates ere I have been granted even the opportunity to fortify myself with my morning coffee anything but gratifying. Nor can I recommend beginning one's day with a vaporish female on the verge of hysterics or a pretentious, toadeating jack-a-dandy as being in any way conducive to sanguinity. Do you always have such an unsettling effect upon those with whom you come in contact, Miss Waincourt? If so, it is not marvelous that you have chosen to isolate yourself in the country, and I can only wonder what whimsy of fate induced you suddenly to inflict yourself upon your cousin's house party."

"No more than I have wondered at it, Your Grace," Miranda uttered in accents of loathing. "But I can assure you that you have cured me of any illusions I might previously have entertained that I should find anything remotely desirable in entering the frivolous circles of polite society. I should far rather remain in the stables than consort with a conceited, overbearing, puffed-up swell whose only redeeming virtues are the ability to tie a neckcloth in the Mathematical and a sublime ignorance of women."

"To the contrary, Miss Waincourt," said the duke gratingly, a dangerous gleam igniting in the hooded eyes, "I may indeed be a fribble, but I have never since I left my shortcoats been ignorant of women."

Miranda stifled a small gasp as His Grace loomed suddenly over her. Hastily backing a step, she came up hard against the great oak desk and found to her discomfort that she could retreat no farther. Having on two previous occasions witnessed that particular look in the duke's eyes, Miranda reached for a handsome

Bilston traveling enamel inkwell complete with pen-holder that sat on the desk behind her.

"Come no closer, Your Grace," she warned in a low, slightly quivering voice and raised Aunt Agatha's prized inkwell threateningly over her head.

No sooner were the words out than Eversley clasped her to his chest with such pent-up fury that Miranda lost her grip on the makeshift weapon. The inkwell crashed to the floor to shatter into a multitude of pieces. Miranda uttered a startled scream cut short by the duke's enraged kiss. It was thus that Aunt Agatha, roused from her sleep by the sounds of battle, burst into the library to discover Miranda struggling in the arms of an elegantly attired stranger and the Bilston ceramic inkwell that had belonged to the late earl's father in ruination upon the floor.

"Miranda!" she uttered in accents of horror. "You have shattered the Bilston inkwell!"

"You, sir, are an unspeakable cad!" hissed Miranda, having been released from Eversley's embrace at her aunt's propitious intrusion.

"Indubitably," the duke uttered, a trifle winded from his recent exertions. "And you, Miss Waincourt, are a prevaricator and a hypocrite."

"Oh!" Miranda exclaimed, beside herself with anger as she swept the room with a searching glance for something to throw at her tormentor. "I loathe and despise you!" She spotted on the mantlepiece a cameo glass spill vase that had belonged to the Waincourt family for four generations.

"Miranda. No!" Aunt Agatha shrieked as she beheld her niece, livid with rage, reaching for the family heirloom "The Staffordshire lion, if you must throw something," she suggested, then in an apologetic aside to the handsome stranger, "I do beg your pardon—er...?"

"Eversley," he supplied with a sudden glitter of amusement. "Your servant, ma'am."

"A pleasure, I am sure," Aunt Agatha responded with a fleeting attempt at a curtsy. "Oh, my! Do look out, Your Grace!" she cried as Miranda let fly the Staffordshire lion with unerring accuracy.

The duke, a renowned athlete, stepped agilely to one side as the china figurine sailed past his head to crash against the wall behind him. Without a moment's hesitation, he straightened and bounded for Miranda, who was even then reaching for a Meissen porcelain urn.

"I think not, my love," he uttered between clenched teeth and wrested the intended projectile from her grasp, upon which she swung at him with a punishing left. Eversley ducked and came up for the clinch, which should have brought the matter harmlessly to an end, had not fate in the form of the "almost insignificant rent" in the Oriental rug taken a hand. Catching the toe of his boot, His Grace stumbled forward, dragging Miranda over backward with him.

"Look, Bertie! There's another one after Manda," cried a childish voice from the open French doors. "Quick! Turn Hann'bal loose!"

"Bertram, no!" a woman shouted.

Eversley, recognizing the voice of doom, stiffened and shot a hasty glance over his shoulder. Too late. The dissolute Hannibal, confronted so unexpectedly by temptation, was seized with an irresistible impulse. Head lowered and feet flying, he struck with the awesome force of a battering ram.

Miranda, suddenly finding herself not only in an undignified heap on the floor, but pinned in a most unseemly manner beneath the erstwhile target of Hannibal's iniquity, stared blankly into the stunned countenance of His Grace of Eversley, white-lipped and speechless with rage. It was only as Bertie made a wild dash after the infamous Hannibal, who, having finally spotted an avenue of escape, bounded through the open French doors followed by a gleeful Allie, and as Aunt Agatha, moaning something about their having become candidates for Jack Ketch, collapsed, swooning, in Miss Melbourne's arms, that the absurdity of the entire situation finally struck Miranda.

So it was that Eversley, recovering in a measure from the shock of having been ignominiously assaulted from behind, gazed into lovely green eyes brimful with hardly suppressed mirth. For a moment their glances looked in sudden understanding, and then they both burst into convulsions of laughter.

It was only after he had managed to catch his breath that the duke discovered that Miranda had grown suddenly quite still and that a blush tinged her cheeks quite charmingly.

"Your Grace," she murmured in a low voice, glancing uneasily toward the door. "If you don't mind? Someone might come in and find us in what might be construed a—well, a rather compromising situation, if you know what I mean."

His Grace was thus recalled to the fact that Miss Waincourt was most delectably held prisoner beneath him and that, furthermore, her sweet lips were poised at a most enticing proximity to his own.

"I know exactly what you mean, my love," he answered quite steadfastly but, to her growing discomfort, made no discernible move to release her. "However, it seems we shall just have to chance it. For until you can be brought to call me something other than 'Your Grace' or 'my lord Duke'—'Evan, darling,' for instance—I fear I simply cannot oblige you."

Quite naturally taking exception to the duke's nefarious means of making sure of his odious wager, Miranda stiffened, her lips parting to indulge him with any number of names, none of which, however, was remotely synonymous with "Evan, darling." But before she could utter even one, he had rendered her mute with his lips pressed to hers in an apparently most disconcerting manner, for though Miss Waincourt, the adamant spinster, did indeed at first struggle, she discovered, as the duke's kiss grew gradually more tender, that her arms had become inexplicably entwined about Eversley's neck.

And then Miss Charity Graves, her sallow face unwontedly animated with livid emotion and a broom clutched vengefully in her clenched fists, burst in upon them.

"I warn you, Miranda," she cried in obvious fury. "A period shall and must instantly be put to that dreadful beast. I have but just now caught him at my herb garden again!"

Eversley, lifting ominously bored eyes to survey the vision of enraged spinsterhood poised on the threshold of the French doors, seemed unimpressed.

"Can it be, my love, that you are somehow acquainted with this extremely odd and ill-mannered person?" he queried with imperiously raised eyebrow.

Miss Graves, at last becoming aware of Miss Waincourt clutched in the arms of a *man* in what only could be described as an attitude of total abandonment, grew even more livid.

"So *this* is how you conduct yourself in private, Miss Waincourt," she exclaimed, drawing herself up in self-righteous indignation. "Millicent Hargrove's daughter sporting on the floor with an out-and-out scoundrel! Why, it does not bear considering. And to think I should have been duped into promoting your suit with my poor, misguided brother."

Miranda, struggling between hilarity and dismay, choked back a helpless gurgle of laughter.

"*Evan, darling*," she said with only a trace of a smile, "I am pleased to present Miss Charity Graves. Miss Graves, the Duke of Eversley."

"Oh, Your Grace!" sputtered Miss Graves, growing rigid with shock. "I never dreamed that—I mean, I had no notion that Miss Waincourt was entertaining so distinguished a visitor. You must know that Miranda's late mother and I were always of the very closest. Consequently, I have felt toward Miranda as if she were my own." Then, apparently remembering the niceties, the bedazzled Miss Graves attempted a belated curtsy, which was made rather awkward by the broom she had frantically sought to conceal within the folds of her black bombazine skirts.

No doubt it was the judgment of the gods that the demoniacal Hannibal should choose then to make his reentrance. Presented with a second opportunity at self-abnegation, the creature was no less fallible. Miss Graves, like the duke before her, was sent flying.

CHAPTER FOURTEEN

SOME THREE DAYS LATER the Duke of Eversley stretched lazily and, drawing his new duchess most satisfyingly against his shoulder, smiled reminiscently.

"You know, my love, that I am perfectly resigned to welcoming into my previously tranquil existence Allie, your two young and probably reprobate brothers and the totally delightful, if somewhat henwitted, Aunt Agatha. Although I confess I still do not perfectly understand why, if she was well aware that the devious child was safe with her governess, she sought to keep it from you."

"Oh, but she didn't," said Miranda, laughing. "For she was quite sure she had made everything exceedingly plain to me. And had I not been so tired and worried about Allie, I do not doubt I should have understood that she was never anxious about Allie's safety, but about my shattered reputation, for which she, the poor dear, blamed herself."

"Quite possibly you are right," replied the duke, willing to concede the point for the time being. "However, I am compelled to profess some doubts as to the advisability of permitting Allie to continue her infatuation with an obvious commoner. Hannibal, it is quite clear, is possessed of a totally unregenerate character and will most certainly come to a bad end.''

"Oh, no, Your Grace." Miranda choked. "How can you say so? When he has had the undeniable good sense to know a toadeater when he sees one. No doubt he will prove invaluable in future as a deterrent to any who might be similarly inclined.''

The duke, much struck at this previously unconsidered possibility, admitted that perhaps the unregenerate Hannibal did indeed have one redeeming quality.

"And now, *Your Grace*," he added significantly, "concerning this matter of your regression: I thought I had cured you of constantly referring to me by my title. After all, you did succumb once to calling me 'Evan, darling.'''

"Oh, but my lord Duke," replied the irrepressible duchess, "you must know that once it became clear to me that I was inescapably compromised and so must marry you, it was imperative that I should submit to your demand. For you must know I am considered a wholly sensible female, and as such I simply *could* not allow a prime stud like Agincourt to be lost on a wager.''

"Jade!" he said feelingly.

"Oh, dear." Miranda sighed with an air of world-weariness. "Are we back to that again?''

"Baggage," he added, a gleam igniting in the dangerously torpid eyes.

"I cannot think, Your Grace, that that is at all the manner in which one should address a duchess of the realm," mused Miranda, lifting her left hand that she might view the exquisite emerald and diamond band glittering on her ring finger. "But then, I have not been acquainted with the dissolute practices of those of the Carlton set. No doubt you shall have to instruct me how to go on."

"No doubt," growled the duke and, enclosing her in a crushing embrace, proceeded without delay to administer the first lesson.

"Oh, Evan *darling*," Miranda said, sighing, upon being released no little time later. "Cousin Tess was quite wrong about you, you know. You are not at all like a great, sleepy pussycat."

ATTRACTIVE, SPACE SAVING BOOK RACK

Display your most prized novels on this handsome and sturdy book rack. The hand-rubbed walnut finish will blend into your library decor with quiet elegance, providing a practical organizer for your favorite hard-or soft-covered books.

Only $9.95

Approximately 16" x 8" when assembled

Assembles in seconds!

To order, rush your name, address and zip code, along with a check or money order for $10.70 ($9.95 plus 75¢ postage and handling) (New York residents add appropriate sales tax), payable to *Harlequin Reader Service* to:

In the U.S.

Harlequin Reader Service
Book Rack Offer
901 Fuhrmann Blvd.
P.O. Box 1325
Buffalo, NY 14269-1325

Offer not available in Canada.

BKR-1

Take 4 novels and a surprise gift FREE

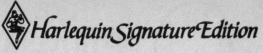
Harlequin Signature Edition

Violet Winspear

THE HONEYMOON

Blackmailed into marriage, a reluctant bride discovers intoxicating passion and heartbreaking doubt.

Is it Jorja or her resemblance to her sister that stirs Renzo Talmonte's desire?

A turbulent love story unfolds in the glorious tradition of Violet Winspear, *la grande dame* of romance fiction.
